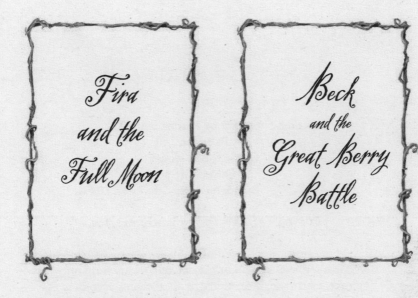

Fira
and the
Full Moon

Beck
and the
Great Berry
Battle

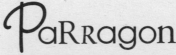

PaRragon

Bath · New York · Singapore · Hong Kong · Cologne · Delhi · Melbourne

First published by Parragon in 2008
Parragon
Queen Street House
4 Queen Street
Bath BA1 1HE, UK

ISBN 978-1-4075-2218-0

Printed in UK

All About Fairies

IF YOU HEAD towards the second star on your right and fly straight on till morning, you'll come to Never Land, a magical island where mermaids play and children never grow up.

When you arrive, you might hear something like the tinkling of little bells. Follow that sound and you'll find Pixie Hollow, the secret heart of Never Land.

A great old maple tree grows in Pixie Hollow, and in it live hundreds of fairies and sparrow men. Some of them can do water magic, others can fly like the wind, and still others can speak to animals. You see, Pixie Hollow is the Never fairies' kingdom, and each fairy who lives there has a special, extraordinary talent.

Not far from the Home Tree, nestled in the branches of a hawthorn, is Mother Dove, the most magical creature of all. She sits on her egg, watching over the fairies, who in turn watch over her. For as long as Mother Dove's egg stays well and whole, no one in Never Land will ever grow old.

Once, Mother Dove's egg *was* broken. But we are not telling the story of the egg here. Now it is time for Fira's and Beck's tales...

Disney fairies

Fira and the Full Moon

FIRA STUMBLED UP THE STAIRS to her bedroom in the Home Tree. Her wings dragged on the ground. Her fairy glow had dimmed to a faint glimmer.

Fira was a light-talent fairy. Usually, she glowed especially brightly. But today she felt too tired to use extra light energy. She felt too tired to fly. Too tired to do anything.

She yawned and stretched her arms wide. Fira had been working hard lately. All the light-talent fairies had. It was a busy time of year. The bushes and plants in Pixie Hollow were bursting with berries and seeds. Harvest-talent fairies worked late into the night, gathering the plentiful crops. So the light-talent fairies' special glows were needed more than ever.

There were celebrations and festivals, where light talents put on dazzling light shows and performed shadow-puppet plays. And long after the sun had set each day, Fira and her friends helped light the orchards and gardens as the harvest-talent fairies worked.

Just that day, the fairies had finished the harvesting. Overflowing baskets filled the Home Tree kitchen and pantry. The work was done. Now Fira was looking forward to a long nap.

Finally, Fira reached her room. Kicking off her petal shoes, she flopped face-down on her bed.

The late-afternoon sunlight shone through Fira's bedroom window. Even though she was ready to sleep – *more than ready*, Fira thought – she didn't close her pine-needle blinds. A light-talent fairy always liked to have a little sunshine brightening a room.

Fira slipped under her dandelion-fluff blanket. All around Pixie Hollow, she knew, Never fairies were working and playing. Cooking-talent fairies prepared the evening meal in the Home Tree kitchen. Art-talent fairies painted and sculpted in their studios. Wing-washing talents cleaned fairies' wings. Fairies milked the dairy mice in the dairy barn and herded caterpillars in the field.

Not me, Fira thought. *I'm not doing anything.*

She closed her eyes. Before she had another thought, she fell fast asleep.

Knock! Knock!

Fira flew out of bed, bumping her head on the ceiling.

"What?" she cried. "What is it?"

"I'm sorry, Fira." Spring, a message-talent fairy, poked her head through the open window. "I didn't know you were sleeping. You're needed at the Firefly Thicket."

Fira sat down on her bed. "What's going on?" she asked sleepily.

"I'm not sure. But there's some sort of firefly trouble."

4

Spring gave an apologetic wave and took off.

"Firefly trouble," Fira repeated. That didn't sound good.

Each night, a group of specially trained fireflies flew around Pixie Hollow. They landed on tiny torches, giving light to the fairies and sparrow men.

These fireflies were Fira's responsibility. She took pride in training them well. She liked being in charge. But just this once, maybe, she could ask Luna or Iridessa to take over. It would be so nice to keep sleeping.

No, no, no. Fira shook her head. *If you want something done right, you should do it yourself,* she thought. Not that she didn't trust her friends. Of course she did. But still…

She sighed. If only she could rest a little while longer. Light-talent fairies' glows were weakest when they were tired. Fira hated it when her glow was dim. She liked to light up a room. Maybe her short nap had been enough. She stood and gathered her strength.

Then she flew out into the afternoon. Fira slowed as she got close to Havendish Stream. The Firefly Thicket was in a dense, leafy spot along the far bank. Fira darted around a clump of bushes. Then she spied the entrance, a wide opening in the branches.

"Hello?" she called softly. She ducked her head inside. It was always dark back there. That was why the fireflies liked it.

"Moth!"

Moth was Fira's nickname. Other fairies

joked that she loved light like a moth loved a candle flame.

"Over here, Moth." Beck, a friend of Fira's, waved her over. Beck was an animal-talent fairy. She could communicate with all the animals in Never Land.

"I'm glad you're here, Fira," said Elixa, a healing-talent fairy. "You need to know what's going on."

Fira gazed around. The fireflies rested fitfully on branches. Their lights flickered dimly. Some didn't light at all.

Beck patted the wings of one firefly. Elixa placed a leaf compress on another.

"They have the no-fire flu," Elixa explained. "They won't be able to light Pixie Hollow tonight."

Fira groaned. It was almost dusk. Already the light-talent fairies would be hanging glow-worm lanterns. But the lanterns were only decoration. The fireflies did the real work of lighting Pixie Hollow. This was trouble, indeed.

Beck went to her side. "I know you're tired from all the harvesting," she said quietly, trying not to disturb the fireflies. "But is there anything you can do?"

Fira straightened her wings. "Of course there's something I can do!"

She would organise all the light-talent fairies. They would need to light the places fireflies usually brightened: gardens, groves, busy sky routes. And the next night a full moon would be out, which meant there would be a dance in the fairy circle. The light-talent fairies would have to light that, too. There was so much work! She had to get going!

With a quick wave goodbye, Fira set off once again. Her mind raced with details. Which fairies would light the fairy-dust mill? Which ones would cover the forest? And who would light the fairy circle?

It was a lot to ask of fairies who were already tired. *It will be all right*, Fira told herself. *We can manage for now. But what if the fireflies are still sick tomorrow?*

2

FIRA DID DOUBLE DUTY that night. She directed light-talent fairies to all corners of the Home Tree. She guided others to locations around Pixie Hollow: the dairy barn, the fairy-dust mill, and the fairy circle, where celebration-setup fairies were preparing for the Fairy Dance.

The next day, Fira slept until mid-afternoon.

"I can't remember ever sleeping so late!" she said out loud. Usually, she woke with the dawning sun. "But I worked so hard last night. I must have been exhausted," she added.

Fira felt a little dazed. *Maybe some food will help*, she thought. *I hope there are some leftovers from lunch.* She was ravenous!

A few minutes later, she flew into the tearoom. Sunlight streamed through floor-to-ceiling windows. Just looking at the sunshine made Fira feel better. She stood for a moment in a bright spot, drawing strength from a sunbeam.

The large room was empty of fairies. Dining tables stood bare, without any food in sight.

"Looks like I'll have to wait for dinner." Fira sighed. She hadn't had anything to eat since dinner the night before. *Maybe I'll just sit right here,* she thought. *No use leaving and coming back.*

Then she smiled. One by one, other light-talent fairies straggled into the tearoom. They walked slowly, rubbing their eyes.

A cooking-talent fairy stuck her head

around the kitchen door. "They're here!" she announced. "The light-talent fairies are here!" Serving-talent fairies hurried out, carrying trays of steaming hot acorn soup and poppy puff rolls.

"They've been waiting for us!" Luna said. She sat next to Fira. "How nice!"

At a nearby table, Iridessa yawned. Then grinned. She sipped the soup happily. "I'm really waking up now!" she giggled.

"Me too," Fira agreed. She took a bite of a roll. "Thank you!" she called to the cooking- and serving-talent fairies.

Fira looked around at the other light-talent fairies. They were perking up but still seemed tired. The night before had taken its toll.

"All right," she said. "I've been thinking about tonight."

"Tonight?" Luna groaned. "I just woke up. Can't we relax for an hour?"

Fira shook her head. "There's too much work to do." She counted on her fingers. "We have to check on the fireflies. We have to figure out new lighting spots. Havendish Stream was much too dark last night. But I have another plan."

"*I* have a headache just thinking about doing it all again!" Iridessa put in.

"I know it's hard," Fira admitted, "but– "

"Everyone!" Spring, the message-talent fairy, darted into the tearoom. "A laugh is coming. It's almost here!"

A laugh! Fira drew a quick breath. She knew what Spring meant. Everyone did. A baby Clumsy – a human baby – had laughed for the very first time. And the laugh was so strong, so magical, it was coming to Never Land, where it would become a Never fairy.

Fira couldn't hold in her excitement. She jumped up quickly. An arrival!

And what if the arrival was a light-talent fairy? Another fairy to help light Pixie Hollow! Fira hardly dared to hope. It would be so wonderful.

Of course, there were so many talents. So many fairy groups deserved to have another member. What were the chances?

"Do you know where it's going to land?" she asked Spring.

"In the orchard!" the messenger said. She was already flying off to deliver the news elsewhere.

Fira grabbed Luna's and Iridessa's hands. "Let's go!"

3

AS THE THREE LIGHT-TALENT fairies flew to the orchard, they were joined by more and more fairies. Beck drew up beside Fira. "Moth, have you heard? This laugh is supposed to be special."

"Aren't they all special?" Vidia said snidely. She was always poking her wings into other fairies' business, trying to stir up trouble.

Beck blushed. "Of course."

Prilla appeared beside them, grinning widely. Prilla had an unusual talent. In the blink of an eye, she could travel to the mainland, the world of Clumsies. Fira had seen her do it. She'd get a strange, glassy-eyed look and wouldn't seem to see anything or anyone. Then, all at once, she'd snap back to Pixie Hollow, with tales of the children she had just visited.

"I just saw this baby!" Prilla told the other fairies. "It's the jolliest Clumsy, so happy and always smiling. Everyone's been waiting for her to laugh. She's been saving it, though, for weeks and weeks. But she finally did it! She laughed! It's sure to be something extraordinary!"

"Hmmm," said Vidia as the fairies landed in the orchard. "Then the new arrival must be a fast-flying fairy. Everyone knows we have the most extraordinary talent."

"With you being the most extraordinary of all?" Fira retorted. Oops! She bit her lip. That snippy comment had just slipped out. Fira usually tried to think before she spoke. She tried not to say or do things in such a hurry that they came out wrong. But it wasn't always easy.

Dozens of fairies and sparrow men hovered eagerly in the orchard. Fira waved to Tinker Bell, a pots-and-pans-talent fairy; to Lily, a garden-talent fairy; and to Orren, a mining-talent sparrow man.

It seemed as if every talent had come. And each fairy hoped that this new arrival would belong to his or her talent group.

Then, suddenly, they all felt it: a slight shifting of the air. Everyone stopped. A wavery shimmer floated above their heads.

A murmur went through the crowd. "The laugh! The laugh!"

The laugh hung above the leafy tree branches for a moment. Then it flew down and settled on the soft green grass.

The shimmer burst apart. And there, before them, sat the arrival.

She rose to her feet, quick and sure. The leftover shimmer of laughter fell around her. It turned into her arrival garment, a soft-as-mist dress.

Fira squeezed Luna's hand tightly. This was it! The arrival was going to make her announcement. She would tell everyone her talent.

"I'm a light-talent fairy." The young fairy spoke loudly and clearly. "My name is Sparkle."

A sigh went through the crowd. Fira hugged Luna and Iridessa. A new light-talent fairy! What luck!

"Fira! Look!" Luna said urgently.

There, above their heads, a second shimmery light hovered in the air.

"Two arrivals!" Fira gasped. She turned to Prilla. "Are they from the same laugh?"

Prilla nodded. "I told you this laugh was amazing."

All around Prilla, fairies and sparrow men whispered excitedly.

The laugh broke apart, and a sparrow man stood before them. He had long golden curls, just like his sister, Sparkle. "My talent is light," he announced. He smoothed a stray hair back into place. "And my name is Helios," he added.

Two light talents! Fira clapped her hands with joy. This was double the luck!

Vidia shook her head. "I'm so happy for you, light-talent fairies," she said. "You need all the help you can get."

Prilla nudged Fira, her eyes shining with wonder. "Look over there!"

Fira gazed into the distance. Then she saw it. A brightening. A soft twinkle. The air pulsed with energy.

Prilla laughed out loud.

Fira thought, *It can't be!*

But it was. The crowd of fairies and sparrow men stood in stunned silence as the laugh exploded in a shower of light. In its place, a young fairy sprawled on the ground. She stretched her wings in an awkward way, knocking into Vidia, who had leaned in for a better look.

"Watch it!" said Vidia, jumping back.

Fira chuckled.

But then the new fairy found her footing and rose. "My name is Glory," she said.

Fira held her breath.

"I am a light-talent fairy!" Glory

told them.

A cheer rose through the crowd. Luna and Iridessa danced with joy. Fira stood for a moment, not moving. Three arrivals, all light talents. This was truly unheard of.

Vidia flapped her wings and took off. "Three young fairies to train," she called out to Fira. "Triplets! I don't envy you one bit."

Fira laughed. She didn't believe that for a second.

The triplets stood close together. They gazed around, taking in everything.

"Just look at them!" Fira told her friends. "They're so well behaved."

They weren't testing their new wings, or trying to fly before they were able.

Fira remembered her own arrival. She hadn't been able to stop spinning around and around, fluttering her wings. She kept trying to get off the ground before she even had her magic.

Terence, a dust-talent sparrow man, flew over to the triplets. He sprinkled a teacup of fairy dust on each one.

That will do it, thought Fira. *They have their magic now!*

The triplets began to glow lemon yellow, edged with gold.

"Their glows are very bright," Prilla said.

"And strong, too," added Beck. It was good fairy manners to compliment the new arrivals.

Still, the young fairies didn't move. The crowd whispered, growing nervous. But Fira grinned. They were taking their time, being careful with their magic. *Good for them,* she thought. They were thinking things through.

Then, with a whoop, the three fairies shot high into the air. Everyone cheered. The triplets zipped. They zoomed. They somersaulted and cartwheeled.

The cheers faded as the triplets flew faster and faster, chasing each other. "*I'm* flying here. You go over there!" Sparkle ordered the other two.

She darted into the leaves of a goldenrod plant. "But, Sparkle!" Helios followed her. "I want to play in the flowers, too. See how they match my hair?"

Glory trailed behind, her flying bumpy and uneven. Helios and Sparkle laughed. "Look at the baby. She can't keep up!" they teased.

Glory burst into tears. She wailed

so loudly, Beck clapped her hands over her ears.

Then all three fairies were pushing and bumping one another, yelling as loudly as they could.

"What a racket!" said Prilla.

"Uh-oh," Fira murmured.

The triplets were out of control.

The crowd of fairies and sparrow men broke up. Some went over to Fira and the other light-talent fairies. They shook their heads with pity and patted them on the back. A few said, "Congratulations." But Fira thought they really meant "Good luck."

If somebody didn't do something, the triplets would be fighting all day. Fira took a deep breath. She tried to smile at Luna and Iridessa. She would take charge. "I'll bring them to the Home Tree and show them around," she offered.

The other light-talent fairies nodded quickly. "Let us know if you need any help," said Luna. She hurried off with Iridessa.

"I will," Fira said, but they were already too far away to hear.

She turned to the triplets. "I'm Fira," she told them. "I'll take you to your rooms."

"Fly with you!" they cried in unison, offering the fairy greeting. They crowded around Fira. Each one tried to get closer than the others.

"This way," Fira said. She squeezed between Sparkle and Helios. Rising into the air, she set out towards the Home Tree.

She smiled at the arrivals flying beside

her. They'd be such a help to the light talents. Sure, they seemed a bit wild. But it was nothing she couldn't manage.

Fira felt sure of it.

4

IN THE HOME TREE, Fira and the triplets looked at the directory in the entrance hall. "Here you are," said Fira. "Your room is on the fourth floor."

"*Room?*" Helios repeated. "Does that mean there's only one?"

"We have to share?" asked Sparkle.

"All three of us?" Glory squealed in dismay.

"It's only until the decoration-talent fairies can get two more rooms ready," said Fira. "Besides, it'll be fun. You'll be right next door to me."

They flew together to the triplets' room. Fira opened the door, and the three young fairies crowded inside.

The decoration-talent fairies had been

busy. One moon-shaped fan hung from the ceiling. But Fira noted that there were three of everything else: three beds, stacked one on top of the other. Three walnut-shell chest of drawers with star-shaped knobs. Three mirrors in a row. Each reflected light from a different window, and each one was larger than the next.

"Here we are!" Fira said.

"I get the top bunk!" Sparkle called.

"No, I want the top one!" said Helios.

"No, me!" cried little Glory.

But Sparkle was already sitting on the bed, swinging her legs. "I'm oldest. I choose first."

"All right," grumbled Helios. "You can have it. But the mirror closest to the light is mine." He stopped to admire himself.

"I wanted that one!" Glory whined. She spun around. "But I'm going to choose a chest first." She raced to the chest of drawers in the far corner.

"Ha-ha," Sparkle teased, flying faster. "Beat you!" She pulled open a drawer.

"Not fair!" screamed Glory. She caught sight of the biggest window. "I'll open the shade," she declared.

"No, me," said Helios. He darted forward.

"I want to," Sparkle called out.

All three dashed towards the window at once.

"Hold on!" Fira stepped in front of them. "I'll get it."

She snapped the shade open.

"I'll get the other ones!" said Sparkle.

"No, wait!" Fira said. She wanted their

crazy contest to end. "Look outside. There are the mining-talent fairies."

Fira pointed out of the window, to the roots of the Home Tree. In a shady corner, two mining-talent fairies were cleaning their tools.

"Let me see!" Sparkle rushed to the window.

"Me too!" Helios flew next to her. Glory tried to squeeze in between them. Giving up, she fluttered up and down, looking over their heads.

"What strange fairies!" exclaimed Helios.

"They just look a little different from the other fairies," Fira explained. "Because mining work needs less flying than other talents, their wings are smaller. And mining-talent fairies are usually shorter, closer to the ground. So they are more comfortable in the mines."

"And their clothes!" Helios said. He smoothed his arrival garment, which was brand-new and brightly coloured. "They look like rags!"

"Not quite like rags," Fira scolded, a little sharply. "They must be getting ready to go mining. And why wear your best clothes if you'll be covered in dust and dirt?" She turned back to the window and leaned out halfway.

"Hello, Precious! Hello, Orren!" Fira called down.

The fairies shaded their eyes and looked up at the window. Neither one smiled.

"Are you going on an expedition?" Fira asked.

"Of course we're going," Precious replied.

"There's a full moon tonight," Orren said grumpily.

Sparkle tapped Fira on the shoulder. "Why don't they sound more excited?"

"Well, that's just their way," Fira said. She wasn't really paying attention. The mining-talent fairies had reminded her of the firefly flu. Usually, the fireflies settled on miners' helmets to light the tunnels. Would they be well enough to help by that night?

She leaned out again to explain the problem to the miners. "I'm not sure any light-talents will be able to guide you. We may need to light Pixie Hollow. Maybe you should hold off," she finished.

"Hold off?" Precious scowled. "Wait a

day? But we always go on the night of the full moon. Always."

"She thinks our work can wait," Orren grumbled. "She thinks that Pixie Hollow doesn't need iron or metal. No, no, no." He shook his head. "Don't mind us. We're just mining-talent fairies. Not important at all. Not like other talents."

"I don't think that," Fira hastened to call down. "I'm– "

A loud crash sounded behind her. Fira spun around. A shattered vase lay on the floor. Miniature sunflowers were strewn among the pieces. Water seeped everywhere.

"Glory did it!" said Sparkle.

"Helios did it," said Glory.

"Sparkle did it," said Helios.

"It doesn't matter who did it," Fira

said. "You need to be more careful."

She helped the triplets clean up the mess. Firefly trouble or no firefly trouble, she had to get these young fairies outside. They needed to use up some energy.

"Come on!" she told them. "I'm giving you a tour of Pixie Hollow!"

Fira and the triplets hovered just outside the Home Tree. *Where should we begin?* Fira wondered. *What would keep them interested?*

"Moth!" Tinker Bell flew out of her workshop. The shop was really an old Clumsy teakettle. Tink had magically transported it to the Home Tree and squeezed it inside. Its door stood under a steel awning, which was actually the spout turned upside down.

"I was just coming to get you!" Tinker

Bell said. "I've come up with a new teakettle for you. It has a few surprises I think you'll like."

Fira grinned. She loved to drink tea in her room each morning while watching the sun rise. *What could this new kettle do that any old one couldn't?* she wondered.

"Come inside!" Tink told her.

Fira glanced at the triplets. Maybe it wasn't a good idea to bring them inside quite yet.

Tink caught her look. "Are the triplets giving you any trouble?" she asked.

"Not a bit." Fira tossed her head. She didn't want Tink to think that three brand-new fairies were getting the better of her.

"Let's go, Sparkle, Helios, Glory!" she

called. "Here's the first stop of our tour!"

"Why do you always call Sparkle first?" Helios demanded. "Do you like her best?"

"Why do you always call me last?" Glory said tearfully.

They kept arguing as they followed Fira and Tinker Bell inside. "Not one bit of trouble?" Tink asked.

Fira laughed. "Well, all right. I'll admit it. Maybe just a bit."

It wasn't just the arrivals that troubled her, of course. It was all that light-talent planning...and the miners' expedition... and the fireflies. Fira really had a lot going on.

Not too much, she told herself. *Just a lot.*

Tink and Fira flew to a corner of the shop. Fira's kettle sat on a worktable, next to a pile of dented trays.

"Is it okay if the triplets take a look around?" Fira asked Tinker Bell.

Tinker Bell frowned, then nodded. "Just don't touch anything," she told the young fairies.

She turned back to Fira and put the kettle over the fire. "When the tea is ready," Tink explained, "steam comes out the spout in different colours."

"Really?" Fira peered at the kettle. It looked exactly the same as any old teakettle. But with Tink's pots-and-pans magic, you never knew what could happen.

Across the room, Sparkle picked up a small frying pan. "Tink said no touching!" Glory reminded her.

Sparkle dropped the pan quickly. It

clanged on the ground.

"But what's this?" Sparkle pointed to a drawing on the handle. It was a tiny pot with squiggly lines for steam rising from it.

"That's my talent mark," Tink told her. "See my initials? T.B.?"

The triplets crowded around. They squinted to see the letters. "Oh, yes!" said Helios. He looked around. "This strainer has your talent mark, too."

"And each piece in this silverware set!" added Glory.

The triplets twisted and turned, checking under handles and inside pots. They were careful not to touch a thing.

Fira smiled. They really were trying.

"Can you show me how this kettle works?" she asked Tinker Bell.

Tink nodded and said, "When the tea

is ready, the kettle whistles and steam comes out, just like always. But the steam is coloured. And each colour is for a different kind of tea. Watch this now."

Just then, the teakettle whistled. A bright orange cloud came out of the spout. "Orange is for thirst-quenching tea," Tink explained.

The colour changed to bright red. "A fiery red steam is for early-morning, just-waking-up tea."

Next, the steam turned a light shade of blue. "And soothing baby blue is perfect for a night-time cup of tea."

While Tink was talking, Fira sneaked glances at the triplets. Their backs were bent over a worktable. They seemed to be studying a big metal sheet. Fira couldn't see much. But they were quiet. They weren't arguing or knocking things over. They were fine.

"Would you care for a nice cup of orange tea?" Tink asked. The steam changed back to orange. She cleared a space at a table and poured two cups. The friends sat down together.

Fira took a sip. "Mmmm! Delicious!"

Tink wrinkled her nose.

"You don't like it?" asked Fira.

Tinker Bell shook her head. "It's not that. Do you smell a funny odour?"

Fira sniffed. There was a definite burning smell in the workshop. What could it be?

The triplets!

At the very same moment, Fira and Tinker Bell turned to the triplets. A cloud of black smoke enveloped them.

In a flash, Fira raced over. "Are you okay?" she yelled, waving away the smoke.

"We're fine," Sparkle said in a quiet voice.

Tink let out a little shriek. "But my brand-new triple-shine copper isn't!" she wailed. She held out the sheet. A giant hole had been burned right through its centre.

"Um, um," Helios stuttered. "We were making sparks... "

He snapped his fingers to show Tink. A bright spark flew from his fingertips.

"To try to burn our own talent marks," Sparkle went on, "and – "

"And we got a little carried away." Glory hung her head.

"The metal is ruined!" Fira was horrified. How could they have been so careless? "I'd fly backward if I could," she told Tinker Bell, apologising in the fairy way. "I feel responsible."

But Tinker Bell barely heard. She moved the sheet this way and that. She tugged on her fringe, deep in thought.

"All I have to do is thin this piece out here…bring the extra metal there…," Tink said, already lost in her repair job. She was too caught up in fixing the sheet to even tell Fira that everything was all right.

"I'd fly backward, too," Sparkle said.

"I'd fly further," Helios said.

"No, me! I'd fly backward furthest," Glory shouted.

"Shhh! Let's leave Tinker Bell to her work." Fira pushed the noisy triplets out of the door.

They were back where they had started, outside the Home Tree. Fira ran her hands through her hair. Now what in Never Land could she do with them?

5

THE THREE YOUNG FAIRIES clustered around Fira. They peppered her with questions and demands.

"What should we do next, Fira?"

"Where can we go?"

"I want to see mermaids."

"I want to visit Tinker Bell again."

"I want to go to the fairy-dust mill!"

"Stop!" Fira practically shouted. She took a deep breath. "I'll tell you where we'll go."

It was a hard decision. Tink had been a good sport about the mishap in her workshop. In fact, she seemed happy to have a problem to fix. Still, Fira would have to think carefully before she brought the triplets anywhere else.

What would be a nice, quiet place? A soothing place, where everyone could relax?

A garden! Fira decided. One with sweet-smelling flowers, shady nooks, and pretty plants. And why not take them to her favourite garden in all of Pixie Hollow? Lily's garden.

"I know just the place," Fira told them. "This way."

She led the triplets past the Home Tree. They flew over a hedge of raspberry bushes. And there was Lily's garden.

A blanket of sweet clover covered the ground. Rows of lilacs and Queen Anne's lace stood in shady groves. The triplets stared. For once, they were speechless.

Fira grinned. She'd made the right choice! Then she spied Lily standing by a young flower.

"You can do it!" Lily whispered to the flower. "You can grow big and strong."

"Wow!" said Fira quietly. She flew closer. "I've never seen that kind of poppy before."

Lily smiled. "It's my first blue poppy! It's doing great. It just needs a little encouragement." She turned to smile at the triplets. "New visitors! Fly with you."

"I'm showing them around Never Land," Fira explained. "And of course we had to stop here."

"Come," Lily said. "You can see my wild rose...and my Queen Anne's lace... and my... "

Fira sat in the shade of a daffodil while Lily led the triplets to each grove and patch of grass. The young fairies were busy. That was good. Fira could take a break and turn her attention to other problems. The fireflies and their flu, to start with.

It was getting late in the day, and the sun was low in the sky. What if the fireflies still weren't feeling any better? The mining-talent fairies would be setting off in just a few hours. They'd need light.

Fira decided she should check with Elixa, the healing-talent fairy. Maybe she'd had some luck finding a cure for the flu.

Wait! Fira sat up straight. Lily's garden had all sorts of herbs and special plants. They could be used for medicine! Were the fireflies trying any of those?

"Lily!" Fira called. She flew over to a wild rosebush. The triplets were measuring their wingspans against a petal.

"My wings are almost twice the size of

a rose petal!" Sparkle said proudly.

"Well, my wings are, too," Helios declared. "And just as soft."

"How about me? How about me?" Glory hopped up and down.

"Have you heard about the firefly flu?" Fira asked Lily above their voices. "Has anyone been here to pick plants for a healing potion?"

Lily nodded. "I've been away on a seed hunt. But Elixa came while I was gone. She left a note saying that she took some herbs. She could be using them for the fireflies."

"Really?" Fira brightened. "Can you show me?"

The two fairies flew off. "Stay there," Fira shouted back to the triplets. "We'll be right back."

Lily took Fira to the far corner of the

garden. They landed in a sunny grassy patch. "Elixa chose mint leaves from right here," Lily said.

Fira studied the plant. She didn't know much about mint, but maybe it would do some good. "How much– " she began. Then she realised that Lily's face had turned ashen.

"What is it?" Fira asked, panicked. "What's wrong?"

"I'm not sure," Lily said. "One of my flowers is upset. I can feel it." She closed her eyes. "It's…it's…it's my brand-new poppy!"

Lily rushed away, with Fira close behind. "This has nothing to do with the triplets." Fira tried to convince herself. "They wouldn't hurt a flower!"

But then she saw the three young fairies

by Lily's new blue poppy. They were glowing their brightest.

"We're having a contest," Helios said, "to see whose glow the flower likes best."

His glow grew brighter. The poppy stretched towards his light, as it would towards the sun.

"Ha!" said Sparkle. "My glow is stronger." She blazed with light. The poppy leaned away from Helios and towards her.

"No fair!" said Glory. "You two are bigger!" She frowned in concentration. She began to glitter and shimmer. The flower twisted in her direction.

"Stop!" Lily cried. "The poppy is exhausted! Please leave it alone."

"Dim your glows," Fira commanded.

The daylight seemed to darken as the triplets obeyed. Lily hovered by the poppy.

"There, there," she said soothingly. "It's all over. You'll be right as rain in a few minutes."

"Did we do something wrong?" Glory asked, confused.

"We? Maybe it was just you!" said Sparkle. "You went last!"

Glory began to cry.

"I'd fly backward, Lily," Fira apologised. "I should have been watching them more carefully."

"It will be all right." Lily spoke in that same cooing voice. But this time, she was looking at Fira.

"Come on. Let's go," Fira told the triplets, "before we do any more harm."

They left Lily still tending her poppy. Fira fluttered her wings, unsure of what to do next. She really needed to check on the fireflies. But what about the triplets?

The three fairies looked at Fira hopefully. Fira sighed. The Pixie Hollow tour wasn't working out anyway. She should take the triplets back to their room. And while she was at the Home Tree, she could stop and see Elixa in her potions workshop. Maybe Elixa had some good news.

"All right," said Fira. "I'm taking you home."

"Why? What are you doing now?" Sparkle asked. "Are you going to your room, too?"

"Uh, no. I have some business."

"Light-talent business?"

"Can we go, too?"

"Can we? Can we?"

The sun was beginning to set. The

mining expedition would be leaving in just a little while. It would take too long to argue with the triplets. It would be faster to let them come along.

"Okay," Fira said. "But this time, stay out of trouble!"

THE POTIONS WORKSHOP was on the third floor of the Home Tree. The door was wide open.

Fira knocked. Then she flew in, followed by the triplets.

The young fairies gazed around the room. Rows of birch-bark shelves filled the workshop from ceiling to floor. Each shelf was crammed with potions, medicines, and plant extracts. Each jar was clearly labelled.

"'Ground-up pine nuts,'" Sparkle read. "'Laurel-leaf bits.' 'Sesame oil.'"

"Elixa?" Fira called. She flew up and down the rows.

"Let's open the jars and smell what's inside," Sparkle whispered to the others.

She twisted off a top. "Ugh! Peat moss."

Glory and Helios started to open jars, too.

"Don't do that," Fira warned, flying back.

"'Right-on-thyme powder. Very fine,'" Helios read, flying to a top shelf.

Sparkle picked up the jar. "Glory, you should try this!" she called. "You're always last. You're never on time." She pretended to toss it to the younger fairy.

"Stop!" Fira hissed. She took the jar out of Sparkle's hands and put it back on the shelf.

"Is there any skin cream here, I wonder?" Helios said as he sorted through more potions in a corner.

"This is a workshop," Fira said. "We really have to be careful."

"Okay," Glory agreed. She spun around clumsily, knocking over a jug marked MUSHROOM POISON! STAY AWAY!

Fira caught the bottle just before it hit the ground.

"Elixa?" she called loudly, and a bit desperately. "Are you here?"

"Yes!"

Fira jumped. Elixa had stepped out from behind a potted miniature raindrop cactus. She wore a light green smock, with lots of big deep pockets, and long gloves.

"I didn't mean to scare you," Elixa said. She smiled at the triplets. "I was so busy working. I didn't realise you were here."

Elixa held up a tube made from a plant stem. One end was stuck into the prickly cactus. "I'm extracting cactus juice."

"Is this part of a potion for the firefly flu?" Fira asked. "Along with the plants from Lily's garden?"

Elixa nodded. "I'm going to mix this with some ground-up mint. It should be an equal blend. One part soothing herb. One part sharp cactus medicine that gets right to the point of healing. Come look."

Fira hesitated. "Oh, the triplets will be fine," Elixa said, as if reading her mind.

Fira wasn't so sure. But she really wanted to examine the healing potion. "Stay still," she ordered the triplets.

She ducked behind the cactus with Elixa. They both sat down, and Fira sighed. It felt good to rest. "See? Here comes the juice now," Elixa said. "I'll just give a careful squeeze to this part of the cactus. There!"

"When will it be ready?" Fira asked.

"Oh, not too long now," Elixa said. "Maybe another hour."

"Another hour? You mean the fireflies will be better soon? They can light Pixie Hollow tonight? And go on the mining expedition?"

Fira felt a burst of energy. Her glow flared. Things were beginning to look up.

Elixa sat back on her heels. She carefully placed the healing potion on a worktable. "Well, the fireflies can take the medicine right after it's finished. But I'm not sure how long it will take to work. It might be a few hours. It might be a few days."

"But tonight is the full moon! The expedition leaves no matter what."

Boom! The cactus gave a sudden jerk.

Its spines shook. The plant stretched higher. It was growing!

"What's going on?" Elixa darted around, unsure of what to do.

With another jerk, the cactus grew a bit more.

"The triplets!" Fira said. She raced around the plant to find the three fairies.

Silently, Glory held out an open jar. "'Growing powder,'" Fira read.

"I wanted to grow," Glory admitted. "But I dropped some onto the cactus by accident."

"Silly little fairy," said Sparkle. She reached for the jar.

"Maybe it will work on my hair," said Helios, reaching, too.

As Glory pulled back, the others leaned forward. The jar tipped over. The rest of the powder poured onto the cactus.

The plant shot up, knocking over jars and shelves. Its sharp spines scraped the walls. Fira grabbed the healing potion from the worktable just before a fast-growing spine knocked it over.

Fira flew towards the ceiling, trying to outrace the growing cactus. The cactus stretched towards her. The workshop shook with the force.

"I can't go any higher!" Fira cried when she reached the ceiling.

Afraid, the triplets pressed themselves against the wall. But the cactus spines kept coming…closer and closer still, as the plant grew.

"We're going to get poked!" Glory shouted. "We can't escape."

The fairies squeezed themselves into a

corner. Glory gasped as a cactus spine pricked her clothes.

"Stay calm," Elixa ordered. She reached into a pocket of her smock and took out a small potions kit. "I always keep an emergency stash handy," she said.

She quickly mixed some green and red powders together. Then she soared between the needles, sprinkling the powder over the cactus.

The plant jerked again. Then, slowly, it began to shrink.

"Whew," said Elixa. "That was close."

Fira helped the triplets out of the corner. But the laboratory was a disaster. Broken jars littered the floor. A layer of spilled powder covered tables, chairs, and shelves. Cactus spines stuck out of seat cushions and through potion recipe books.

Everything was in shambles – again!

"We'll help clean up," Sparkle offered. "Right, you two?" she said to the others.

Glory and Helios nodded. "Do you have any extra smocks?" Helios asked. "I don't want to get my clothes dirty."

Elixa shook her head. "I think you're better off leaving things alone. This is a delicate job. Potions might get mixed together, and that could be trouble. Really, only healing-talent fairies should help."

"I'd fly backward," Fira said for what felt like the millionth time that day.

Elixa shrugged. "That's okay."

Fira held up the healing potion for the fireflies. "At least we still have this."

Elixa eyed the triplets, then took the jar. "I'd better hold on to it."

Fira agreed. "We'll leave now," she said. She turned to the triplets.

But they were already gone.

7

THOSE FAIRIES! FIRA THOUGHT. *First Tink's metal. Then Lily's flower. Then the mess at Elixa's workshop. And now they've flown off without a word. Who knows where they could have gone?*

She tried to think calmly. But her mind was racing. Sparkle had wanted to see the Mermaid Lagoon. Fira would start there.

But only the mermaids were at the lagoon, singing mermaid songs and combing their hair.

Next, Fira visited the fairy-dust mill, the dairy barn, and Havendish Stream. The triplets were nowhere to be found.

It was getting dark now. Not knowing what to do, Fira flew home. Her wings felt heavy. She yawned.

Finally, she flew into the first floor of the Home Tree. Up she went through the holes in the ceilings, climbing floor by floor. She knew she had lots to think about. The triplets still needed to be found. And then there were the fireflies. What would happen to Pixie Hollow and the mining-talent fairies if the fireflies still had the flu? Fira needed to make some plans.

But right now, all she wanted was to lie on her bed, close her eyes, and rest.

She flew past the triplets' room.

Soft sounds escaped through the keyhole. Fira stopped short. They'd been there all along! If only she hadn't been so hasty. If only she hadn't wasted time scouring Pixie Hollow from one end to the other. She could have been napping instead. Of course, she should have tried their room first.

She burst into the bedroom.

The three sat close together on one bed. They looked up, happy to see Fira. "You're here!" said Sparkle. "We've been waiting for you!"

"We made such a mess of things. We didn't want to go anywhere else," Helios explained.

"What can we do to make things better?" Glory asked.

Was there anything they could do? Fira hesitated.

Just then, Spring, the message-talent fairy, flew in behind her. "I have a message from Elixa," Spring told Fira. "The fireflies are feeling better."

"Thank goodness!" Fira clapped

her hands.

"But their glow is still weak," Spring went on. "They might not be able to light Pixie Hollow for the whole night."

Fira drooped. Once again, the light-talent fairies couldn't rest. Just in case the fireflies lost their glow, the fairies had to be ready to fill in.

"The fireflies can't guide the miners, either," continued Spring. "It's too risky."

No fireflies on the expedition? No light-talent fairies who could leave Pixie Hollow?

That left Fira – and Fira alone – to lead the miners.

An hour later, Fira sat in her room. She gazed at the full moon, drawing strength from its light. She'd already helped the light-talent fairies find their places around

Pixie Hollow. She'd even made a schedule for them. Now it was almost time for the expedition.

Fira knew she was taking on a lot. After all the flying and chasing and fairy-sitting she'd done that day, she already felt tired. But she had to be strong. She was in charge. And so many fairies were counting on her.

She got up to leave.

Knock, knock, knock.

"No fair." Sparkle's voice came through the door loud and clear. "I told you I'd knock first."

"But you always go first," Glory complained. "Why can't I knock first?"

Helios said, "Knock, snock. Let's just go in. I'm sure Fira will be glad to see us. Are my wings straight?"

Fira opened the door. "I was just on my way out," she told them.

"We need to say something first," said Sparkle. She stepped in front of the others.

Fira glanced at the moon. Time was running out. "I know you feel bad about everything that happened," she said to the triplets. She tried not to sound impatient. "You've told me already. But I really need to go. The miners need me."

"We know. We want you to take us with you," Sparkle said. "We can help."

"Yes!" said Helios. "You didn't give us an assignment for tonight. All the other light-talent fairies have one."

"You don't trust us," added Glory, "because we made such a mess of things." She jumped up and down and hit her head against the doorframe. "Ouch! But we have lots of light energy. We can really help…if you'll let us."

Fira stared at the triplets. For a moment, she thought maybe they could help her with the mining trip. But then she remembered everything that had happened. Of course they were too young and too inexperienced to go.

"The best way for you to help is to stay in your room," she told them. "Don't go anywhere. Don't do anything. Don't even talk to anyone."

Without another word, she darted out of the window. As she flew, she could hear the triplets.

"This is all your fault, Glory."

"No, it's not. It's your fault, Sparkle. You're always so bossy."

"What about Helios? He never pays attention. Stop looking in that mirror, Helios!"

But soon their voices faded away. Fira flew on, alone.

8

THE NEVER MINE WAS DEEP in the woods. The entrance was a cave in a small clearing.

Fira flew there quickly. She soared through the night in the light of the full moon.

Outside the mine, Precious, Orren, and the other miners waited. One mouse stood ready, a mining cart harnessed to his back. The cart was empty. But the miners hoped to fill it with Never iron, pewter, and other metals. Another mouse carried sacks filled with axes, spades, and picks.

Fira landed next to Orren. "I'm here," she said, "ready to light the tunnel."

Just then, a large cloud covered the moon. The woods darkened, and Fira shivered.

"All right, Fira. It's time to go," Orren said in his gloomy voice. "Everyone, form a line. Fira, you should go first."

One by one, the fairies, sparrow men, and mice entered the tunnel. Fira brightened her glow. The tunnel was wide, but its ceiling was low, so the fairies had to walk instead of flying.

By the light of her own glow, Fira could see bits of wood shoring up the cave ceiling. Clouds of dust danced around her feet. The miners plodded through the tunnel with heavy steps.

"We'll need to go far into the cave," Precious said from behind Fira. "All the ore has been mined near the front."

Still, the mining expedition continued at the same slow pace. The fairies crept like snails through the tunnel. Bit by bit, the path narrowed. It dipped deep underground. It twisted and turned, splitting in two again and again.

"Left," Orren directed Fira. "Now right. Take that tunnel. The one with the steep stairs."

This is more complicated than any maze, Fira thought. *I'm glad Orren knows the way!*

Not one glimmer of light seeped into the mine from outside now. The air felt cool.

They went further and further into the tunnel. Water dripped from the walls. Fira hugged herself for warmth and turned up her glow.

Her step was slowing. Her bones felt weary. She was glad when Orren said, "Stop. I have to check the map."

She rested a moment, directing her

glow so that Orren could read. "We're almost there," he said. "Crystal Cave is just ahead. Past there, we should find new ore."

Orren squinted. "Can you glow a bit more brightly?" he asked Fira. "Everyone needs to be able to see."

Fira concentrated. Her light blazed more strongly.

"Thank you," Orren said gruffly.

A few moments later, they stepped into a large cavern. Fira spun slowly. Glittering gems lined the walls. They reflected Fira's light with brilliant reds, greens, and blues. Fira felt refreshed, as if her wings had been washed with cool water on a hot summer day. Her glow brightened.

"Beautiful, isn't it?" Precious said. Her voice sounded lighter to Fira. Almost happy.

Precious reached out and touched one of the gems. Fira could tell that Precious loved these rocks, just as Fira loved light. They were her joy. Fira gave Precious an understanding smile. Precious smiled back. Then she added in her gloomy way, "But we need to keep moving."

The expedition trudged forward. "Here it is," announced Orren. Fira stopped. They stood in another large opening. But this cavern had no jewels. Its walls were smooth and bare.

"We can begin," Orren told the others. Each miner took a tool.

Fira sat in the centre of the chamber. She cast her light into one corner, then another. She tried to brighten each spot in the cavern.

If they mine as slowly as they walk, Fira

thought, *we'll be here until the next full moon.*

But the miners were as quick as lightning. They struck the walls with picks. They hacked away at stones with axes. They shovelled bits of ore into the mouse cart.

"Try this area!" Precious directed. "Go deeper over there!"

Fira drew on all her strength to keep the room lit.

In just a little while, the cart was filled. "Our job is done," Orren said. "We can go."

The group started retracing their steps. Fira slipped on a stone and faltered. She righted herself. But something was wrong. Her glow was dimming. Full moon or no full moon, she felt more tired than she'd ever felt before.

I can't keep up my glow, she thought.

After a few more steps, they entered Crystal Cave. Fira hoped that the bright gems would help her once again.

Whoosh! A sharp gust of wind blew through the cavern. It hit Fira full force. She shook with the chill.

"Oh, no!" she moaned. Her glow flickered, then went out.

The jewels shone dimly. Fira guessed that the gems were picking up bits of light from the low, dim glows of the miners.

"Too dark," said Orren. "Can't make out much of anything."

"Not even the way out," Precious said with a shrug.

"We can't leave Crystal Cave!" Fira cried. "We can't go anywhere at all!"

They were trapped!

9

"UH-HUH," ORREN AGREED with Fira. "We're stuck, all right."

"Looks like we're goners," Precious added in a flat tone.

The other miners shuffled their feet. Some sat, leaning against big rocks. One miner twiddled her thumbs. Another scratched an itch.

Orren poured cups of water for everyone from a chestnut-shell flask.

Nobody panicked. Nobody cried out in fear. They settled on the ground and accepted their fate. Even the mice stood quietly.

"I'm not giving up!" Fira said.

But what could she do? They were so

far underground. So far from light.

The only thing she could do was rest...and see if her glow came back.

She found a corner where the gems twinkled the most brightly. Sitting back against the wall, she closed her eyes.

A heaviness settled over her wings. She felt herself drift. Seconds passed, then minutes. Finally, Fira sat up with a start. Had she even slept? She didn't think so. She was too anxious.

"Feeling better?" Orren asked.

Fira wasn't sure. A blast of cool air blew through the cavern. She shivered. She hadn't felt cold when the expedition had kept moving. But now that they were staying in one spot, she felt chilled to the bone. Her stomach rumbled with hunger.

"I'll try to glow now," she told Orren.

Fira took a deep breath. Her glow flickered, strong and bright. She grinned. It was working! But then, as if a switch had turned it off, the light snuffed out.

Fira took another breath and tried with every inch of her being to glow.

Nothing happened.

"This is all my fault!" she cried. "We're trapped here because of me."

Orren patted her back. "There, there. We knew the danger. We wanted to go. We are at fault."

Fira knew that it was useless to place blame. But she couldn't help scolding herself.

"Oh, why did I come on my own?" she asked herself aloud. "I could have taken another light-talent or two. But no, no. I was so sure I could do this alone, without anyone's help. And now we're all in real trouble." She put her head in her hands.

"There, there," Orren said again, awkwardly. "Someone will come looking for us. Eventually."

"Eventually." Fira sighed. How long would that be?

Fira and the miners fell quiet. In the silence, Fira heard a noise. It sounded like a giggle.

Was she imagining things?

Tee-hee.

It *was* a giggle!

"What?" A few miners raised their heads.

"Shhh!" Fira held a finger to her lips. Now she heard voices. Three different voices, talking to one another. Arguing.

Could it be?

Nature

You'll be
amazed at the vast
variety of fauna and flora
in Pixie Hollow! What's more,
the Fairies live in complete harmony
with the *beautiful* world around them. Some
fairies can even speak to the plants
and animals!

The **dazzling** sunlight, rich soil and soft
raindrops of Pixie Hollow help the Never plants
and flowers to grow. Plus, garden-talent fairies
can talk to the shrubs of Pixie Hollow and will give
them all of the encouragement they need to be able
to bloom into healthy and happy plants.

Cute and friendly animals also live in Pixie Hollow.
The animal-talent fairies make sure that every
creature is **happy**; these special fairies can even
speak to the animals in their own language!

Fairies aren't the only incredible creatures in
Pixie Hollow, so get ready to learn more.

And remember… believing is **just
the beginning!**

Flowers

Did you know that it's not only garden-talent fairies that absolutely **adore** flowers? Flowers are a friend to every fairy - whether it's offering them a home, a quilt to keep them warm at night or even a stunning dress.

Pixie Hollow is blessed with hundreds of different types of **vibrant** and colourful plants and flowers. You'll find *beautiful* buds and *blossoms* by the side of streams, in meadows, clinging to the side of great trees or simply sitting in a well-kept fairy garden.

Here are some examples of the ways in which Never Fairies use flowers every day.

Shelter
Flower petals are a fantastic material for constructing fairy houses. Whether woven together or alone, flower petals are waterproof and a good insulator – plus they look fabulous!

As a Friend
Garden-talent fairies can often be heard whispering their secrets to the flowers in their gardens. Not only can garden-talent fairies understand how a plant is feeling, but plants have a pretty good understanding of these special fairies too, which makes them great friends.

Fashion
Violet wrap dresses, blue tulip bubble skirts and woven ivy bonnets – Never Fairies love to make clothes out of flowers.

Food
The flowers of Pixie Hollow collect sweet dew on their petals and leaves overnight, which is a particularly tasty treat for the fairies. Pollen is also collected from flowers and used to sprinkle on cakes or desserts. Sweet pollen can also be used to stir into warm buttermilk, making it sugary and syrupy!

Animals

There are so many different species of animals that live in Pixie Hollow; it's impossible to name them all! But here are just a few *crazy* creatures for you to read about...

Never Mice

Mice are raised by Never Fairies for their wool and milk. Some fairies even have a special talent for grooming and milking mice. Mouse cheese is a delicious snack, especially when it's eaten with poppy seed crackers!

Saber Fish

These water-dwelling creatures have teeth longer than their fins! This breed of friendly fish get on very well with water fairies despite their **strange** appearance.

Tiffins

Tiffins are odd-looking creatures that live in the Banana-Tree Forest. They have ears like **elephants** and bodies that are half the size of humans – so they tower above fairies! Tiffins sometimes trade their bananas with the fairies.

Hawks

These powerful predatory birds are a danger to fairies. Fairy scouts are constantly on the lookout for hawks, and if an alarm is sounded, every fairy *immediately* flies for cover. Hawks live the other side of the Wough River, which is just outside of Pixie Hollow.

Trees

Home Tree
The most famous tree of them all is the Home Tree, a towering maple tree in the heart of Pixie Hollow. The source of *magical* Pixie Dust, this tree is very special to the fairies. Fairy workshops are located in the lower stories of the tree and a winding staircase leads from the first floor to the second.

Bimbim Tree
This tree's roots can survive the *fiercest fire*! This is a truly magical type of tree, which can only be found in certain parts of Never Land, such as Pixie Hollow.

Cuddle Vine

This **pesky** plant is so affectionate; it grabs hold of anything that passes near it! These over-friendly plants get on really well with Garden Fairies, they're the only ones who don't find the Cuddle Vine a little too friendly. If you get too close it might just grab you and never let go!

Possum Ferns

This is a very rare, silvery green plant with tightly coiled, velvety leaves. A Possum Fern has a personality all of its own, and when it feels startled it *'plays dead'* by uncoiling its leaves and turning brown. There aren't many of these plants in Pixie Hollow and fairies sometimes like to play a game where they count how many they can spot.

Take the Fairy Nature Test!

What nature-themed hobby would suit you best?
Take the test below to find out.

1. What is your favourite thing to watch on TV?
A. ~~B.~~ Programmes about birds
~~B.~~ B. Programmes about science
~~C.~~ C. Nature shows about fluffy mammals
D. Flower shows ✓

2. What kinds of books do you like to read?
A. Books that make you concentrate hard
B. Books that make you use your memory
C. Storybooks ✓
D. Books that give you beauty tips

3. When are you at your happiest?
A. When you're sitting quietly
B. When you're counting or doing maths ✓
C. When you're being friendly and helpful to others
D. When you're making the world around you look beautiful

Answers:
- *If you scored mostly As then you'd enjoy bird watching.*
- *If you scored mostly Bs then you'd enjoy counting Possum Ferns.*
- *If you scored mostly Cs then you'd enjoy rearing mice.*
- *If you scored mostly Ds then you'd enjoy gardening.*

The voices grew louder.

"I see footprints over here!"

"No! There are more footprints this way. Let's take this tunnel."

"No, no, no, Sparkle. You think you know everything. This is the way to go!"

It was the triplets! They were right outside Crystal Cave!

"Sparkle! Helios! Glory!" shouted Fira. She had never thought she'd be so happy to hear their arguing.

"Helios! Glory! Sparkle!" she added, to be fair. Then, "Glory, Sparkle, Helios! We're here! We're here!"

10

THE TRIPLETS BURST INTO Crystal Cave. Their glows lit the room with a dazzling brightness.

Fira rushed over to give them hugs. "What are you doing here?" she cried.

Sparkle shrugged. For once, she seemed unsure. "We thought we could help."

"We know we didn't listen to you," Helios added. "You told us to stay in our room. But we followed you. We thought you might have trouble. We thought you really could use our help."

"Yes," Glory put in. "We all agreed. We didn't have one fight about it."

"Our glows are so strong," Sparkle said. "We have all this energy. And you seemed...tired."

Precious stepped closer. "Looks like we're rescued," she said with a sigh.

"Yes," said Orren. "Let's give a cheer."

"Hooray," the miners chimed together in flat voices. "Hooray for the triplets."

"Well, what are we waiting for?" Fira laughed with relief. "Let's get going!"
This time, the triplets led the way. They took turns going first, the other two walking behind with Fira.

"So you're not angry?" Glory asked.

Fira shook her head. "You really rescued us. I should have realised what a help you'd be. I judged you too quickly."

And wasn't I just as rash when I was a young fairy? Fira thought. Even now, she didn't always think everything through. Like the triplets, she was still learning. *After all, a true leader has to work as part of a team.*

The expedition wound its way back through the maze of tunnels. Then, as the sun began to rise, they went out of the cave entrance and into the woods.

"Not much longer now," said Precious in a glum voice. "We're almost home."

A few minutes later, the miners stopped at the dairy barn. "We have to put these mice to bed now," Orren said. "So we'll part here."

Fira hugged Precious. The mining fairy stood stiffly for a moment. Then Fira felt her hug back. "See you in the tearoom!" Fira called to the miners.

But suddenly, she let out a jaw-cracking yawn. She felt too tired for breakfast. Instead, the triplets led her to her cosy room.

"Here," said Helios. He passed by the mirror without so much as a glance. "You get into bed."

"Yes," Sparkle agreed. "Good idea, Helios." She took Fira's shoes off and fluffed up the pillow. Fira lay down. Glory pulled the blanket up to her chin.

"Hey!" said Fira sleepily. "You're still not fighting."

"Maybe we learned something, too," Glory said. "Now you just rest. We'll get you a nice cup of baby blue tea."

"I'll brew it!" Sparkle said eagerly.

"No, it was my idea!" Glory said. "I'll do it!"

"I want to!" Helios rushed to the kettle. "I can make a perfect cup."

The arguing went on and on. But Fira didn't hear a thing. She was fast asleep.

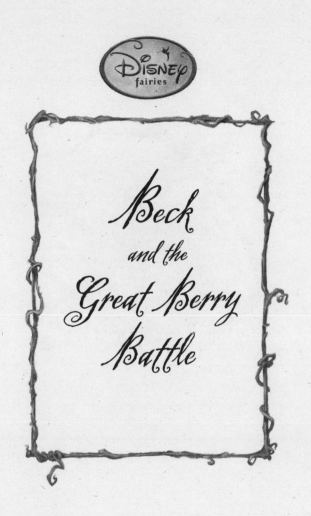

Beck
and the
Great Berry
Battle

A SQUIRREL PERCHED on a log paused while chewing on some seeds. He watched as two tiny Never fairies zipped past him, side by side.

"Oh, Beck," one of the fairies said to the other as they flew. "Thank you so much for coming with me." She looked terribly worried. "We just don't know what to do. A baby raccoon turned up in the gardens this morning, and he ate all the strawberries out of Thistle's strawberry patch. And then he started digging up Rosetta's mint! We chased him off, but he didn't go far. Now he's sitting on a tree stump by Havendish Stream. He won't budge. And none of the other animal-talent fairies can understand a word he's saying!"

Beck smiled. "Don't worry, Latia," she said. They were nearing Havendish Stream. "We'll figure it out."

Latia breathed a sigh of relief. "Well, if any fairy in Never Land *can* figure it out, it's you, Beck!"

Every fairy in Never Land agreed: Beck was one of the finest animal-talent fairies in Pixie Hollow. She loved being around animals, from the tiniest insects to the largest mammals. Oh, sure, snakes could be a little grumpy. Skunks were hard to read. And hawks, of course, were just plain dangerous. But all in all, she loved feeling a part of the animal world. Sometimes Beck secretly wished that *she* were an animal!

Like all the animal-talent fairies, Beck had a gift for talking to animals. Birdcalls, mouse squeaks, squirrel and chipmunk chatter — they were just noises to the other fairies, but to animal-talent fairies, those sounds were as clear and easy to understand as words and sentences.

Beck was especially good at talking to baby animals, perhaps because she was so playful and lighthearted. Even when an animal was too young to speak, Beck could understand it. Queen Clarion said Beck had empathy and could sense animals' emotions. When those emotions were strong enough, Beck felt them, too.

So when a baby raccoon parked himself on a stump and refused to move, everyone thought of Beck right away. The animal fairies sent Latia to fetch Beck because she was a forest-talent fairy and knew the quickest ways to get through Pixie Hollow.

An easy five-minute flight later, the two fairies came to Havendish Stream. A dozen animal-talent fairies were hovering around a tiny raccoon, who sat on a tree stump clutching a stalk of Rosetta's mint.

"Beck's here!" Latia called, and all the fairies turned.

"Oh, thank goodness!" cried Fawn, one of Beck's best friends. She drew Beck closer to the tree stump. "Beck, you've just got to help. This poor little fella won't budge. We don't even know where he CAME from." With a push from Fawn, Beck found herself right in front of the baby raccoon. He raised his head and whimpered.

"Hello there," Beck said in Raccoon. "I'm Beck. What's your name?"

The little raccoon let out another whimper. Then he buried his face in his paws and rubbed his nose in the stalk of mint he had picked from Rosetta's garden.

"Oh, don't cry!" Beck said. She flew up and stroked the top of the raccoon's furry head. The raccoon rocked back and forth. He was so sad and so scared that Beck was starting to feel sad, too. She straightened her back, cleared her throat, and forced herself to cheer up. If she didn't watch out, soon she'd be crying as hard as the little raccoon, and then where would the fairies be?

"Hey, now," said Beck, smiling. "Don't cry, my friend. Why would you cry when you could be playing a game with me?"

Raising his head, the little raccoon looked at Beck for the first time. She smiled encouragingly and patted his nose. "That's right," she said. "I know the perfect game for us to play. It's called Find the Fairy!"

With that, Beck took off at top speed. She looped around behind the raccoon and tapped him on the shoulder. "Here I am!" she cried. The raccoon squeaked in surprise and turned around, but Beck was already gone.

The little raccoon peered up at the sky, trying to find her. Meanwhile, Beck quietly landed by the stump and tiptoed around to the front, where the raccoon's paw rested on the edge. She reached up, tweaked his toe, and cried, "No, *here* I am!" then flew up to face him again.

The little raccoon let out a chittering noise: raccoon laughter. All the fairies smiled at each other. Beck had done it again!

Beck grinned. She was so glad that the little fellow was feeling better. "That's a good game, isn't it?" she said. "Now let's start again. My name is Beck. What's wrong?"

There was a pause, and the fairies held their breath. Then the raccoon replied. To the fairies who didn't speak Raccoon, what he said sounded like "Grak!"

But Beck understood him.

"Lost!" was what the raccoon said. Beck realised that he was so young, he still spoke Raccoon baby talk. He stared at Beck with wide eyes. "Lost!" he said again.

"Oh, dear. Well, where do you live?" Beck asked.

"Live. . . ," he whispered. He looked

down at the mint stalk he still held. He raised his paw and shook the mint at Beck. "Live *here!*" he said. "Live. . .in *mint*."

"Huh," said Beck, switching out of Raccoon. She looked at the fairies who were gathered around. Everyone looked as confused as she felt.

"What did he say?" asked Latia.

"He said. . .that he lives. . .in *mint*," Beck told her. "But that doesn't make any sense!"

"In mint?" replied Latia thoughtfully. "I wonder if he means — Oh, Beck! I know where he lives!"

"Remember when Rosetta planted her mint patch a few years ago?" Latia asked Beck. They were flying through the woods, with the raccoon trailing after them. "Well, she asked me to find her some wild mint seeds from the forest, because she likes their flavour. So I got her some seeds from a big old wild mint patch at the base of a hollow tree right on the edge of Pixie Hollow. I just *bet* his family lives in that tree!"

"You must be right," agreed Beck. "That would explain why he was so interested in Rosetta's mint patch to begin with. It must have reminded him of—"

"*Home!*" cried the little raccoon, and took off running. Beck and Latia looked up, and sure enough, there was the big hollow tree. And playing in the mint leaves at the bottom of the tree was another baby raccoon. She was about the same age as Beck's little friend — who was in such a hurry to get to the tree that he ran straight into her. The two young raccoons tumbled in a heap at the foot of the hollow tree, squeaking happily.

It was obvious that the little raccoon was home.

Soon, it had all been sorted out. Beck explained everything to the baby raccoon's mother, who thanked her again and again.

Beck waved goodbye to the baby raccoon, and then she and Latia flew off in the direction of the Home Tree.

As they were flying over a thicket, Beck spotted Grandmother Mole coming out of an underground tunnel. "Oh, Latia, why don't you go on without me?" Beck suggested. "I want to pay a visit."

Grandmother Mole was the oldest female mole in Never Land, and a very dear friend. She and old Grandfather Mole had no children or grandchildren of their own. But they were known throughout Pixie Hollow as Grandmother and Grandfather

Mole.

"Hello, Grandmother," Beck said in Mole. She landed at the animal's side.

"Beck? Is that you?" asked Grandmother Mole in a series of grunts and nose whistles.

"Yes, it's me," Beck replied. "I was just flying by and I saw you. How's everything underground?"

"Oh, just fine," Grandmother Mole replied.

Just then, old Grandfather Mole climbed out of the tunnel opening — and bumped right into Beck. "Oops!" he said with an embarrassed chuckle. He squinted in Beck's direction. "Pardon me, sir! Wasn't watching where I was going, I guess!" He chuckled again.

Then Grandfather Mole waddled off.

Grandmother Mole giggled at his blunder —
calling Beck "sir." Beck couldn't help
giggling, too. All the moles were
shortsighted. But Grandfather Mole, well, he
was practically blind.

After saying farewell to Grandmother
Mole, Beck flew east, to the Home Tree.

But just as Beck flew over the river, she
heard a cry. A cry for her? Was someone calling her name? As she slowed, it got louder.

"Beck! Be-e-e-e-eck! Wait! Wait up!"
the voice called.

Beck stopped and hovered in midair.

She turned to look behind her — and saw
a young hummingbird headed straight for her,
at full speed. He was screaming at the top of
his lungs. "Beck! Help! He-e-e-e-elp!"

2

THE YOUNG HUMMINGBIRD tried to put on the brakes. But it was too late. He was going too fast. Beck dodged to her right. Unfortunately, the hummingbird had the same thought. He dodged to his left — and smashed right into her.

The crash knocked Beck backwards.

"Twitter!" Beck exclaimed in Bird. She shook her head, trying to clear it. "What in the world is going on?"

Twitter was no stranger to Beck. He was a highly-strung little hummingbird. He was *so* highly-strung that sometimes his mouth had a hard time keeping up with his brain.

"I'm s-s-sorry about that, B-B-Beck!" Twitter chirped in stuttering cheeps and peeps. He nervously darted to and fro in the air. His wings flapped so quickly, they seemed a blur to Beck's eyes. Still dazed from the mid-air crash, Beck was getting dizzy trying to keep her eye on Twitter. He stayed in the same place for only seconds at a time.

"I s-s-saw you f-f-flying by," Twitter said. "And it's j-j-just that you've g-g-got to help us — the hummingbirds. It's an e-e-emergency!"

Now over the shock of bumping into Twitter, Beck smiled. How many times had she heard that word —"emergency"— from Twitter before? Twitter was a sweet, good, and earnest little bird, and Beck liked him very much. But sometimes Twitter got overexcited for no reason.

He came looking for Beck whenever he needed help or advice. Usually, he was in a panic, as he was now. Once Beck found out the facts, she could explain why there was nothing for Twitter to worry about. Beck suspected that this was another one of those times.

She turned and headed east again, beckoning for Twitter to follow. "Come on, Twitter," she chirped. "I'm headed back to the Home Tree. Come with me. Along the way, you can tell me what's wrong."

Twitter hurried after Beck. "B-b-but you don't understand!" he called to her. "You have to c-c-come with me, back to the nest. Quick!"

Beck flew on. It was always a little hard for her to deal with Twitter when he was in a state. His nervousness could be contagious. She *knew* that everything was fine and that Twitter was upset about nothing. But his panic was so strong that it made her heart beat faster in sympathy.

It's nothing, she reminded herself. *He's all upset about nothing. It's never as bad as he thinks it is.*

She knew this from having dealt with Twitter's panicky episodes so many times before. One of the first times had been when Twitter was just a chick. He had seen apple blossom petals falling to the ground and had rushed to Beck in a panic.

"B-B-Beck! Come quick!" he had said. "It's snowing! It's not *supposed* to snow in Never Land!" It had taken Beck a while to reassure Twitter that the petals were just petals.

There had also been the time when Twitter had noticed that all the beautiful round yellow flowers he liked so much had disappeared. "Someone changed them into strange white puffy things," he said. "And they *fall apart*."

Beck had explained to Twitter that they were dandelions, and that was how they spread their seeds. While he didn't like it — not one bit — he had finally calmed down.

So now Beck felt sure that Twitter's "problem" wasn't as big as he thought it was. "Okay, Twitter," she said. "What is it? I'm listening."

Twitter zigged this way and zagged that way in the air. "I'm telling you," he said, "it's an emergency! It's—" Twitter looked nervously over one wing, then the other. He flew right up to Beck's left ear and whispered, "It's the *chipmunks*."

"The chipmunks?" Beck said at a normal volume. "What about the chipmunks?"

"Shhh!" Twitter cringed and went on whispering. "Not so loud! They might be listening. They're everywhere." Twitter shot glances over both wings again. Then he continued. "And they're so grabby and strange. I think they have it in for all us birds. They come right up into the trees and shrubs. They gather all the seeds and acorns and berries in sight. And then, get this: they don't *eat* the stuff. They carry it away with them to their underground nests. You know what I think? I think they're *hoarding* all that food. They're taking it and storing it somewhere — just so the birds *can't have it*." Twitter backed away from Beck's ear. He stopped whispering. "Why would they do that, Beck? Why?"

Beck listened carefully to everything Twitter said. She managed to keep a straight face the whole time. But when Twitter had finished, she couldn't help it. She smiled. Then she giggled.

Twitter was confused. "What's so funny?" he asked Beck. "This is serious! This is an *emergency!*"

Beck fought back another giggle. "I'm sorry, Twitter," she said kindly. "I know you're upset. But there's no reason to be. The chipmunks mean no harm," she told him.

Twitter looked at her doubtfully.

"It's true," Beck went on. "Some animals, like birds, eat food as they find it. But other animals, like chipmunks, store some of the food they find. They save it until they need it. *Then* they eat it."

Twitter looked at Beck in surprise. "They do?" he asked.

Beck nodded. "Mm-hmm. It's nothing personal," she pointed out. "They don't have it in for the birds. They're just doing what they've always done. Besides, there's plenty of food to go around." Beck looked into Twitter's eyes. "Okay?" she asked.

Twitter thought it over for a second. "Okay!" he replied cheerfully. And just like that, Twitter was back to being a carefree little hummingbird. "Thanks, Beck!" he exclaimed as he zipped out of sight.

"You're welcome!" Beck called after him. She shook her head and smiled.

Just as quickly as he had come, Twitter was gone.

3

THAT AFTERNOON, Beck was the first animal-talent fairy to get to the Home Tree tearoom. As she waited for the others, Beck sipped peppermint tea.

She looked around the room. The tearoom was one of the fanciest rooms in the Home Tree. The walls were hung with Never pale-grass wallpaper. The silver chandelier overhead sparkled and shone. The floral carpet was plush and colourful. And during the day, light flooded into the room through the floor-to-ceiling windows.

Beck loved the spot where the animal-talent fairies had their table, right next to one of the windows. She was gazing outside when Fawn sat down next to her. There was a bright purple stain on one shoulder of her dress.

Beck giggled. "What happened to you?" she asked Fawn.

Fawn reached for the teapot in the centre of the table. She poured herself a cup of tea. "A berry fell on me," she explained. "After you took that raccoon home, I went to talk to this chameleon I know. He was feeling a little blue today." Fawn couldn't help smiling at her own silly joke. "Then I headed back here, and just as I landed in the courtyard — *splat!*" Fawn shrugged. "Just bad luck, I guess."

Beck shrugged, too. Never fairies were used to dodging all sorts of things falling from above. Raindrops falling from the sky. Leaves or branches falling from trees. Berries falling from shrubs. They had to be careful. But these things were just a bother — not a big danger. Not like hawks, which could swoop out of the sky and carry away a Never fairy in a split second. That was why the fairies had scouts to watch for hawks. As for berries, they could make a big mess, but they hardly ever fell directly on a fairy.

Terra, Madge, and Finn were the next animal-talent fairies to come to the table. They helped themselves to tea. Dulcie, a baking-talent fairy, flew over with a plate of star-shaped butter cookies. Everyone reached for one at the same time.

"Easy, easy!" Dulcie cried as she flew away. "There's plenty more where those came from."

"That's good," said Finn. She nodded towards the tearoom door. "Because here comes Cora. And it looks like she could use a pick-me-up."

Cora flopped into the last empty seat with a frustrated sigh. It was plain to see what was the matter. Bright purple juice soaked the top of her head, and was smeared on the sides of her face where she had tried to wipe it away.

"You, too, Cora?" Fawn asked. She pointed to the big purple splotch on her own dress.

Cora squinted at Fawn through the purple liquid. "Berry?" she said.

Fawn nodded.

"Yup," said Cora. "It came out of nowhere. Another one almost hit me, too."

Beck wrinkled her brow. "What a strange coincidence," she said. "Two fairies hit by berries in the same day. That doesn't happen very often."

On the other side of the table, Finn

stared at something over Beck's shoulder. "Make that *three* fairies," said Finn.

"Huh?" said Beck. She turned to look.

Sure enough, a sparrow man at the art-talent table had a big purple stain on his left leg.

"I count four," said Madge. Across the room a decoration-talent fairy was wiping purple juice from the back of her neck.

"Uh. . .no," said Fawn. "Five." She nodded in the direction of the tearoom door. Lympia, a laundry fairy, had just flown in. Two purple splotches — one on her right arm and one on her left wing — showed where she had been hit.

What in the world was going on?

"This is no coincidence," said Beck. "Five fairies hit by berries in the same day? In the same *afternoon?*"

Just then, a loud *tap-tap*ping sound made all six animal-talents jump in their seats. They turned towards the window. Outside, hovering, peeking in at them, was Twitter. He tapped again at the window with his long, thin beak.

Madge reached over and swung open the window. Twitter landed on the sill.

"B-B-Beck!" he chirped, short of breath. "Come qu-qu-quick! It's an emergency!"

All the animal-talent fairies smiled at Beck. They knew as well as she did how overexcited Twitter could get.

Madge patted Twitter gently on the head. "There, there, Twitter," she said in Bird. "It can't be all *that* bad."

Finn offered Twitter a cookie. "Here, try one of these," she said. "It'll make everything better."

But the animal-talents knew that Beck was the only fairy with the patience to calm the little bird.

Twitter didn't take the cookie. "You don't understand!" he cried. Twitter hopped off the windowsill. He darted nervously from side to side. "A battle has broken out! B-B-Beck, you've got to do something! You've g-g-got to stop it!"

Beck squinted at the little bird. "A *battle?*" she said doubtfully. Even for Twitter, it sounded like a huge exaggeration — like something blown way out of proportion.

But the next thing Twitter said got the animal-talent fairies' attention.

"Yes, a battle!" he exclaimed. "A *berry* battle!"

4

BECK HURRIED OUT of the tearoom. She zipped through the Home Tree entrance hall and out of the front door. She met Twitter outside the tearoom window.

"Twitter," Beck called to him, "what do you m—" Out of the corner of her eye, she spied a berry falling towards her. She dodged to her right. The berry just missed her left shoulder. "What do you mean, a berry battle?" she asked.

Twitter launched excitedly into a long explanation. But he was chirping almost as quickly as his wings were flapping. Beck could only understand bits and pieces.

"The chipmunks stole the nest!" cried Twitter. Then Beck caught something about the hummingbirds deciding to fight back and "launching berries" and "defending our shrubs" and "keeping the chipmunks away." But the more Twitter explained, the more confused Beck got.

"Okay, okay, Twitter," Beck calmly interrupted him. "Let's do this: why don't you *show* me what you're talking about? Lead the way. I'll follow. And we'll get to the bottom of this together."

Without another word, Twitter turned and flew away. Beck hurried after him. At times, it was hard to keep up with his unpredictable flight pattern.

Twitter would be headed straight for a tree trunk. Then, at the last possible moment, he would zigzag around it. He dodged branches — sailing over some, ducking under others. Beck followed Twitter's crazy path as they headed northeast from the Home Tree.

Before long, Twitter stopped and perched on the branch of a blackberry bush. Beck landed next to him. She looked around. Nothing seemed out of the ordinary. All around them, the forest was perfectly quiet.

Twitter sat silently, staring in front of him. Beck's curiosity bubbled over. "Twitter—" she began.

But Twitter shushed her. He pointed a wing towards the clearing at the foot of the blackberry bush. "Watch," he whispered.

So Beck sat quietly. She watched and waited. Sure enough, in a few moments, a chipmunk scampered out from behind a hawthorn tree. He looked to his left. He looked to his right. He looked up into the trees. Then he scampered across the clearing towards the blackberry bush. In the centre of the clearing, the chipmunk stopped. He sat up on his hind legs. He sniffed the air. Beck could sense his nervousness — and his eagerness. He was determined to get his paws on some of those blackberries.

Suddenly, the blackberry bush seemed to spring to life. It was full of hummingbirds — young ones, old ones, male and female. Beck hadn't even noticed they were there, scattered throughout the bush, high and low.

Beck watched as the hummingbirds worked in pairs. One hummingbird bent back a branch. Another bird balanced a blackberry at the very tip of the branch.

Then, all at once, the hummingbirds let go of the branches. A storm of blackberries went flying in the direction of the clearing. A few went astray. Some hooked to the left, to the right, or backwards. Some flew straight up into the air. Those came plummeting back down towards the blackberry bush. Beck saw one of them hit a hummingbird on the head.

But most of them flew directly at the chipmunk. He flinched as he saw the wave of berries headed right for him. He barely had time to turn away before they hit: one on his tail, one on the back of his head, and three more on his back. Several others were near misses.

Then, dripping berry juice, the chipmunk scampered out of the clearing — back the way he had come. He disappeared behind the hawthorn tree.

"Hooray!" A round of cheerful hummingbird chirps rose from the blackberry bush.

It had all happened so fast that Beck hadn't had time to move. But now, shocked by what she had seen, she leaped off the branch. For once, Twitter was right. This WAS an emergency! Hummingbirds attacking a chipmunk with berries? What was going on here? She flew out in front of the blackberry bush. She turned to face the bush and hovered over the clearing.

"Stop! Stop!" she called in Bird. She held her hands up in front of her. "What are you doing? Why would you do that to that chipmunk?"

"Oh, good day to you, Beck," came a voice from the blackberry bush. Beck peered into the bush to see where — and who — it was coming from. Suddenly, from a low branch, out flew Birdie, one of the oldest hummingbirds in Pixie Hollow. Beck had known her for a long, long time. She was a no-nonsense, plainspoken old bird. "I see you've heard about our. . .*problem*," Birdie said, hovering next to Beck.

Beck shrugged. "Well, yes and no," she said. "I've heard that there *is* a problem. But I don't understand. What's going on?"

Birdie sighed a big sigh. "We have to be able to defend ourselves. Don't we?"

Now Beck was even more confused. "Defend yourselves?" she asked. "Defend yourselves from whom?"

"From the chipmunks, of course," Birdie replied. "They stole one of our nests! One minute it was here — right on one of these very branches." Birdie waved a wing at the blackberry bush. "The next minute it was gone! And a chipmunk was seen sniffing around that branch, just about that same time. All the hummingbirds nearby noticed him."

Beck thought over what Birdie had said. "Did anyone actually *see* the chipmunk take the nest?" she asked.

"Well," said Birdie, "no. But you know what chipmunks are like, Beck. They hoard. They stockpile. They hide away everything in sight. I'm sure they took it. They're very well-made nests, you know."

Birdie's chest puffed out with pride. "Those chipmunks probably want to use it in one of their underground rooms — for padding or something. But they can't do that to us! They can't just steal one of our nests. And until they give it back or say they're sorry, they're not welcome in *our* shrubs. They can't help themselves to *these* berries. And if they get too close. . .well. . .just let them try!"

5

BECK DIDN'T GET very far with Birdie.
She tried. But Birdie wouldn't listen. She
was certain the chipmunks were thieves.

As for the chipmunks, they were just as
certain that the hummingbirds were being
mean. Beck had decided to get their side of
the story. When she found them, the chipmunks were plotting their revenge against
the birds. Uncle Munk, one of the chipmunk elders, and five others were gathered
near the entrance to Uncle Munk's underground home.

Beck tried to get them to calm down.
She told them what the hummingbirds had
said.

"Of course we didn't take their nest!"
insisted Uncle Munk in excited chipmunk

chatter. "What would we want with one of their nests?"

"Great!" Beck replied. "Then it's just a misunderstanding. It can all be settled peacefully."

But the chipmunks were mad. Already, too many of them had been berried.

"Everywhere we go in Pixie Hollow, we get hit with berries," Uncle Munk said to Beck. "We have to gather the food we need. Otherwise, we'll starve. We have to be able to defend ourselves. Don't we?"

With that, the chipmunks went back to their planning.

"Here's what we do," Uncle Munk instructed. "We fan out in all directions. Keeping our distance, we circle the blackberry bush. Then we each start tunnelling underground towards the bush. Oh, it'll be slow going. It could take days, even weeks. But when we get to the roots, we pop up from underground. And we take the berries by force! Let's see them try to stop us!"

Beck couldn't believe what she was hearing. She had to put an end to this before it got entirely out of hand. She knew there had to be a way. But what was it?

Just then, a young chipmunk called Nan came running at full speed around a tree trunk.

"Waaaaah!" screamed Nan as she ran. "Take cover! Take cover!"

Behind her, a shower of berries splattered on the forest floor, just missing her. Nan made a beeline for Uncle Munk's home. She dove headfirst down the entrance. As more berries landed closer and closer to them, the other six chipmunks followed

Nan's lead. Beck was left alone, hovering over the entrance.

She dodged one berry, then another. But a third berry sailed high over her head. Beck watched it as it flew. It carved a wide, high arc in the air, then began its fall back to earth. At the same moment, an old mole came strolling around a tree trunk, directly into the berry's path.

It was Grandfather Mole. The berry dropped right on his head. *Splat!*

Grandfather Mole stopped in his tracks. He reached up to feel his head. Finding it dripping wet, he turned and squinted in Beck's direction.

"Good day, sir," said the shortsighted old mole. "Awfully large raindrops we're having today, aren't we?"

6

GRANDFATHER MOLE'S STATEMENT was not so far off. Because within a few days, it seemed to be raining berries — all over Pixie Hollow, all the time.

Some Never fairies started carrying their flower-petal umbrellas whenever they went outside. But, as every fairy soon found out, dainty flower-petal umbrellas didn't hold up very well to constant berry bombardment.

"Phooey!" said Silvermist, a water fairy, as she flew into Home Tree. Her water-lily umbrella was covered in berry juice. It also had been knocked inside out by the force of some direct hits. Silvermist shook the umbrella as she tried to close it. "This is the fourth umbrella I've gone through in two days!"

Beck overheard Silvermist and flew over to invite her to the umbrella exchange table. She led Silvermist across the entrance hall. There, Rosetta and three other garden fairies sat behind a tree-bark table. "You can drop off your ruined umbrella," Beck explained. "And you can pick up a new umbrella. The garden fairies will use your old one for seeds. So everyone wins!"

The umbrella exchange table had been Beck's idea. The Berry Battle was making big trouble for all the Never fairies, and she felt bad about that. Over the past few days, between visits to Mother Dove, the animal-talents had gone to see the hummingbirds and the chipmunks many times. They had tried to talk sense into them. But neither side was budging.

In the meantime, Beck wanted to do

something to make things easier for the fairies. So she asked her garden-talent friends for help. They were experts at making flower-petal umbrellas, and were more than happy to pitch in. And now the idea of the umbrella exchange table seemed to be taking off.

Beck glanced out of the entrance hall window. She needed to get outside. She needed to check in with the animals. Maybe something had changed. Maybe they had called a truce. Or maybe today was the day Beck would think of some way to get them to stop fighting.

She said goodbye to her friends and flew towards the front door of the Home Tree. Then, at the door, she turned and flew back. She took a daisy-petal umbrella from the new-umbrella pile. "Mind if I borrow this?" she asked Rosetta.

Rosetta giggled. "Of course not," she replied.

And so, armed with the umbrella, Beck ventured outside. Almost right away, she heard a berry splatter on her open umbrella. Beck flew quickly through the berry shower. She dodged berries whenever she could. She only had to go a short distance out in the open — just as far as the big oak tree with the split trunk. From there, she could continue her trip underground by using the tunnels that were part of the animal-talent domain.

Long, long ago — so long ago that Mother Dove was the only one who could remember — the animal-talent fairies had built a huge system of tunnels stretching across Never Land. The fairies used them to get anywhere they wanted, without being seen and without setting foot outdoors.

Like all animal-talent fairies, Beck knew every inch of the tunnels like the back of her hand. But to other fairies, the tunnel system was a baffling maze. It wound through burrows, tree hollows, nests, and dens. A few had been abandoned, but many of them were home to families of animals.

Beck had decided that using the tunnels was the best way to travel while the Berry Battle raged. That way, she could stay dry and free of berry stains.

Beck set out first for the chipmunk camp. Diving through a small hole at the base of the big oak tree, she zipped down an underground tunnel that led towards Havendish Stream. She went above-ground to cross the stream, flying up a hollowed-out section of a maple tree, then down through the centre of a dead branch that spanned the water. Then, back underground, she headed due north through a series of empty fox dens.

On her way through the first den, she met Fawn coming in the opposite direction.

"Fawn!" Beck cried. Her face lit up at the sight of her friend. "I was on my way to see the chipmunks. Is there any news about the Berry Battle?"

Fawn frowned and shook her head. "Nothing good," she replied. "I just came from the hummingbird camp. They're still at it. No sign of either side letting up." Then Fawn's face brightened. "But now that I think of it, there is *one* piece of good news."

Beck's glow flared from her excitement. "I could use some cheering up," she replied eagerly. "What is it?"

"You know the chipmunks' plan to tunnel their way to the blackberry bushes?" Fawn asked. "Well, that plan backfired."

Beck looked confused. "What do you mean 'backfired'?" she asked Fawn. "What happened?"

Just then, they heard a muffled scratching sound. It was coming from the tunnel that led north out of the fox den.

Fawn nodded in the direction of the sound. "That will answer your question," she told Beck.

Puzzled, Beck flew over to the tunnel opening. She peered down the dim passage. The sound was getting louder. . .and closer.

As Beck peered farther into the tunnel, a large paw suddenly punched through the floor. It tore at the edges of the hole it had created, widening the opening. Then a furry head with a longish snout and tiny, beady eyes poked into the tunnel and looked around.

It was Grandmother Mole.

She spotted Beck and Fawn hovering in the doorway to the fox den.

"Oops!" said Grandmother Mole. She turned to talk to someone behind her. "Back up! Retreat!" she said. "False report! This isn't a chipmunk tunnel. It's the fairies' tunnel. Abort mission! Repeat: abort mission!"

Beck was bewildered. She had no clue what kind of "mission" Grandmother Mole was leading. But she had a hunch it had something to do with the Berry Battle. And that could mean only one thing.

The moles had taken sides.

7

BECK'S HUNCH TURNED out to be right. The moles had sided with the hummingbirds in the Berry Battle.

"But why?" Beck asked Grandmother Mole. She and Fawn hovered on either side of the old mole in the dim tunnel. "Why would you want to get mixed up in all this?"

Grandmother Mole snorted. "Well," she said, "we didn't want to. But then those nasty chipmunks started digging all over the place. They started tunnelling around all the blackberry bushes in Pixie Hollow. They bulldozed right through *our* tunnels. That's not nice. Plus, they caused a lot of damage. Our tunnels had to be fixed after the chipmunks ploughed through." Grandmother Mole shrugged. "We had to do *something*."

From the look on Fawn's face, Beck could tell she already knew what that "something" was. Beck was afraid to ask. But she asked anyway. Grandmother Mole explained how the moles had been. . .*fiddling* with the chipmunks' tunnels.

"When they stop digging for the day, we build lots of side tunnels off their tunnels," she said. "They come back the next day, and they get confused. They can't figure out where they left off." Grandmother Mole stifled a giggle. "We've got them so turned around, they don't know which way is up."

Beck sighed. She didn't like the fact that there were now *more* animals involved in the Berry Battle. She shook her head slowly.

"So now it's the hummingbirds and the moles against the chipmunks," she said sadly.

At Beck's side, Fawn cleared her throat. "Actually, Beck," she said, "now it's the hummingbirds and the moles against the chipmunks and the *mice*."

Beck hurried on to the chipmunks' camp near Uncle Munk's home. She didn't want to believe what Fawn had said: that the mice had entered the war, too.

But when Beck reached the chipmunks' camp, she found that it was true. Little Nan, the young chipmunk whom Beck had seen diving for cover into Uncle Munk's home a few days earlier, brought her up to date. Nan was a very shy, quiet little chipmunk. She didn't speak much to the other chipmunks — let alone to the Never fairies. So when she and Beck had first met, many moons before, it had taken Beck a long time to win Nan's trust.

Now, however, little Nan felt as comfortable with Beck as she did with her own family.

"The hummingbirds accidentally hit a baby mouse with a berry," Nan explained to Beck. "Oh, they've hit plenty of other mice. Their aim is not always so good, you know. But this was a baby. The poor thing was completely drenched — and scared. After that, the mice took our side."

Beck pulled Nan aside, away from the worst of the fighting. They sat in the shelter of a hollow log. From there, they could see the animals battling it out.

It wasn't a pretty scene. To their left, the hummingbirds launched berries from the blackberry bush. To their right, chipmunks filled the branches of a hawthorn tree. Mice scurried to and fro in the clearing between.

They collected any berries that fell to the ground still intact. Then, scurrying into the hawthorn tree, they passed those berries off to the chipmunks. The chipmunks balanced those on their tails. Then they flung them back at the hummingbirds.

Beck pointed at a sparrow flying towards the chipmunks in the hawthorn tree. He was carrying a berry in his beak.

"What's that sparrow doing?" Beck wondered aloud.

Nan followed Beck's gaze. "Oh," she replied. "I forgot to mention: the sparrows are on the hummingbirds' side. So are the chickadees and the cardinals."

Beck peered up into the air. Flocks of birds were dive-bombing the hawthorn tree. Berries were flying and falling everywhere. The Berry Battle was getting completely out of hand!

In the midst of it all, little Twitter flew right past Beck and Nan. He was so busy dodging falling berries that he didn't see them.

"Twitter!" Beck called out to him.

Twitter looked around, trying to work out who was calling him.

"Over here!" Beck called. "Inside the log!"

Twitter saw her and flew over to the hollow log. He landed inside, next to Beck. "Phew!" he said, shaking some berry juice off one wing. "It's g-g-getting harder and harder to g-g-get around out there!"

That was when Twitter looked up. He saw Nan standing on the other side of Beck.

"Oh!" said Twitter, staring at Nan. "It's a ch-ch-chipmunk!" he said to Beck.

Beck smiled. She stepped out of the way so that Twitter and Nan could face each other.

"That's right, Twitter," said Beck in Bird. "It's a chipmunk. Her name is Nan." Beck turned and spoke in Chipmunk to Nan. "Nan, this is Twitter."

There was a long, awkward silence. Twitter stared at Nan. Nan stared at Twitter. Their families were fighting against each other. They both felt as if maybe *they* should be fighting. Maybe that was what they were *supposed* to do.

But what do you know? Neither of them particularly felt like fighting.

8

BECK WATCHED TWITTER and Nan eye each other curiously. When their eyes met, they both looked away bashfully. Twitter stared at the ground. Nan tugged at her ear. Then, slowly, their gazes crept towards each other again.

It was Twitter who asked the first question. "Where does she live?" he chirped at Beck.

Beck pointed to the east. "Over there," she replied. "Past the hawthorn tree, over the stream, in a little burrow."

"Where does he live?" Nan asked Beck.

Beck pointed west. "In a big mulberry bush over that way."

"Is he your friend?" asked Nan.

"Yes, he is," replied Beck. "And guess

what? He loves to play hide-and-seek." Beck knew that Nan also loved to play hide-and-seek. And she knew that no one had played any games at all since the Berry Battle had begun.

"Really? Do you think he'd play hide-and-seek with me?" Nan asked shyly.

Beck turned to Twitter. "Nan wants to know if you'll play hide-and-seek with her," she said.

Twitter jumped a few inches off the ground and hovered in mid-air. "Yeah!" he replied. He was so excited, he flew an upside-down loop. Beck didn't have to translate that. Nan understood. She put her paws over her eyes. Twitter flew down to the other end of the log and hid behind a leaf. Nan opened her eyes and started looking. Just as she reached the leaf that Twitter was hiding behind, he popped up and flew off to the other side of the hollow log. Nan followed him.

Beck giggled as she watched them go. Twitter and Nan were so excited about making friends, they had forgotten all about her. She turned and looked out towards the berry battlefield. She sighed. *If only the grown-up animals could put aside their differences as easily as the young ones*, she thought.

In the distance, she spotted Terence, a fairy-dust-talent sparrow man. He was struggling to fly through the shower of berries. In his arms he carried a dried mini-pumpkin jar full of fairy dust.

Terence gave out the daily doses of fairy dust to the Never fairies. Each fairy got one level teacupful every day. It was an important job. Without fairy dust, fairies could only fly about a foot at a time. But with fairy dust, they could fly as long and as far as they wanted.

Beck guessed that Terence was on his way back to the Home Tree from the mill. He was trying to dodge berries as he flew. Beck took off to see if she could help him. But as she did, she saw a large berry fall right on Terence's jar and knock it out of his hands. The jar fell to the ground. Fairy dust spilled everywhere.

"Oh, Terence," Beck said when she reached his side. "Are you all right?"

Terence looked very unhappy. "I'm fine," he answered glumly. "But this fairy dust is wasted." He looked down at the glittery powder on the forest floor. Beck followed his gaze. A thin layer of fairy dust had fallen on an anthill. As she watched, all the ants that had been sprinkled with dust took to the air and flew around. Then she noticed a couple of spiders and an earthworm hovering in the air next to her.

Beck couldn't help laughing at the strange sight. "At least someone's getting some use out of it," she said.

Terence wasn't amused. "Yeah," he said. "But now— Oh, watch out!" He pulled Beck out of the path of a falling blackberry. "Now I have to make another trip back to the mill." He sighed a heavy sigh. "I'll tell you, Beck. This Berry Battle is out of control!"

"You don't know the half of it!" Beck replied. She told Terence about the moles, the mice, the sparrows, the chickadees, and the cardinals. "Now *they're* all mixed up in this silly spat, too!"

Terence shook his head in disbelief. "What do you think would get them to stop fighting?" he asked.

At that very moment, Beck heard Nan and Twitter — or felt them with her animal-talent sense. Later, she couldn't exactly say which. But either way, she knew without a doubt that she had to find them. They needed her — and fast!

Beck wheeled around. She squinted to see across the clearing. Her eyes found the hollow log where she had last seen the youngsters. What she saw made her gasp aloud.

A large hawk was perched on top of the log. He bent over to poke his sharp beak into the hollow interior.

Hiding inside the log, cornered, were Twitter and Nan.

9

BECK SPRANG INTO action. She flew straight for the hawk, across the berry battle-field.

"Hold your fire!" she shouted in both Bird and Chipmunk as she flew down the front lines of the Berry Battle. "I repeat, hold your fire!"

Beck knew she couldn't fight off the hawk herself. She would need help — and lots of it. But none of the chipmunks or hummingbirds had seen that Nan and Twitter were in trouble. So as she flew, Beck waved her arms wildly. She threw herself in front of flying berries. She did everything she could think of to get the animals' attention.

She pointed at the hawk. "Stop fighting and look!" she shouted.

Slowly but surely, the warring animals noticed Beck. Hummingbirds and chipmunks alike froze in the middle of berry launches. A few moles who had popped up from underground watched Beck fly by. Mice looked up from their berry-collection duties. Sparrows, chickadees, and cardinals circled in the air. They were curious to see what Beck was shouting about.

They all looked where she was pointing. They saw the hawk. And they saw Nan and Twitter.

All at once, the Berry Battle came to a halt.

Beck reached the log first. Now she could see why Twitter and Nan were cornered. The hawk had smashed in one end of the hollow log, blocking the exit. That left only the one open end, which he was guarding. He was hunched over, peering upside down into the log. He couldn't go in after the young animals. The log was too small. Instead, he waited for them to try to escape.

Beck didn't stop to think. She swooped past the hawk's face, flying dangerously close to his curved beak. She got his attention. She flew up, behind his head. The hawk sat upright as his eyes followed her. She circled his head. She didn't really have a plan. She just hoped to draw his attention away from the youngsters. If she could distract him long enough, maybe they could get away.

The hummingbirds saw what Beck was trying to do and caught on. Within moments, dozens of hummingbirds swarmed around the hawk. They poked at the top of his head with their long, pointy beaks. They flew in front of his face, zigging and zagging.

Their tactics had an effect. The hawk was getting mad. He lunged at a hummingbird and snapped his beak just millimetres from her wing. He flapped his wings out wide, as if trying to shoo the tiny birds and the fairy away. The wind from the hawk's flapping blew some hummingbirds off course. A few others were hit by his wings and knocked to the ground. They sat, dazed, for a moment before they were able to get up and take to the air again.

But through it all, the hawk didn't budge from the log.

Other birds moved in to take the place of the hummingbirds. Sparrows, chickadees, and cardinals circled over the hawk's head. Then, one by one, they dive-bombed the hawk with berries. Many made direct hits.

Several berries hit the hawk on the head. One hit him right between the eyes.

But the berries didn't bother the hawk. He barely noticed them. They were tiny to a bird of his size. In fact, even as the birds dropped berries on him, the hawk went back to peering into the log.

The animals had to find another way to distract him!

The chipmunks launched the next attack. They scurried onto tree branches hanging directly over the log. Then, throwing caution to the wind, two chipmunks dove onto the back of the hawk's head. He stood bolt upright on the log. He raised his right wing and brushed at his head, trying to get the chipmunks off. The chipmunks clung for dear life. As long as they could hang on to the back of the bird's head, they were safe from his sharp beak and talons.

Meanwhile, behind the hawk's back, Uncle Munk had sneaked up to the log. Hugging one side of it, he crept closer and closer to the open end. Now, while the hawk was distracted, he scurried up to the opening. He peeked around the corner and into the log.

"Psst!" he whispered to Nan and Twitter. "Come on! Follow me! The coast is clear. But we don't have much time!"

Even though he couldn't understand Uncle Munk's words, Twitter zipped forward.

But Nan didn't follow.

"Nan!" Uncle Munk whispered to her from the end of the log. "Come on! Now's our chance!"

Nan was frozen with fear. She couldn't

move. She huddled against the back of the log, trembling, her eyes wide.

"You go ahead!" Uncle Munk whispered to Twitter, waving him on. Twitter hesitated. He looked back and forth from Nan to Uncle Munk. He didn't want to leave his new friend behind. But Uncle Munk was a grown-up. Twitter felt he should do what Uncle Munk wanted.

So Twitter flitted past Uncle Munk and out of the log. The hawk, still trying to shake the chipmunks off his head, didn't even see him fly past. Within seconds, Twitter was safe. He landed on a blackberry branch. The hummingbirds flocked to him to make sure he was okay.

"I'm f-f-fine," he told everyone. "But Nan. . ."

Nan was still trapped inside the log.

Uncle Munk stood at the opening, trying to convince her to make a break for it.

"You can do it, Nan," Beck heard Uncle Munk say. "Just put one paw in front of the other. Come towards me."

He was so focused on Nan, he didn't notice that the hawk had shaken the chipmunks off. They ran for cover as the giant bird turned back to the log. He spotted Uncle Munk.

Beck and all the animals gasped.

"Uncle Munk!" Beck called. "Run!"

Uncle Munk heard Beck. He looked up. The hawk's eyes were glued to him. The bird leaned in. His shadow fell over Uncle Munk. Then, in one sudden, lightning-fast movement, the hawk lunged at Uncle Munk. The chipmunk dodged the bird's hooked beak, wheeled around, and scurried away.

The hawk leaned over to look inside the log once more. Seeing Nan still there, he settled down to wait for her to come out. He showed no sign of giving up.

The animals had to try something else. Birdie the hummingbird had an idea. As Beck had done, she swooped past the hawk's face to get his attention. Then she landed on the ground a few feet in front of the log. She hopped along, dragging one wing behind her. The hawk watched her, cocking his head. He leaned forward to get a closer look.

"She's pretending she's hurt!" Beck said to Uncle Munk. "She's figuring that hawks go for the easiest prey first. Young animals are easy targets. But injured animals are even easier. She's trying to lure the hawk off the log – to get him to go for her."

What Birdie was doing was terribly

dangerous. She was risking her own life to save Nan's.

Beck and Uncle Munk watched as Birdie turned her back on the hawk. Slowly, slowly, she hopped away from the log. The hawk leaned over again to look in at Nan. Then he looked up at Birdie. He looked back and forth between his two choices of prey. He seemed torn — between the trapped chipmunk he couldn't reach and the hurt hummingbird inching away from him. He had to decide.

The hawk spread his wings and leaped off the log. He soared the short distance to Birdie and got ready to drop onto the little bird. But at the last possible moment, Birdie took to the air. She flew a few feet, landed again, and continued hopping along, dragging her wing. The hawk flew after her and pounced again. Again, Birdie took off at the last second. She flew several feet, landed, and hopped. The hawk followed her.

"Now is our chance," whispered Uncle Munk. He sprang into action. With the hawk out of the way, he dashed over to the log. He leaped inside and ran to the back.

"Nan, come with me! You can do it!" he told her.

With a little encouragement and a lot of shoving, Uncle Munk got Nan out of the log. They ran away as fast as they could. Within seconds, they were safe, hidden behind the trunk of an oak tree.

"Birdie!" Beck called out. "Birdie, they're clear!"

Birdie heard Beck's call and knew that Nan was safe. So when the hawk pounced again, she took to the air. This time, she sped away.

The confused hawk watched her fly out of his reach. Then, remembering the trapped little chipmunk, he flew back to the log. Peering inside, he saw that Nan was gone. He checked on both sides of the log to make sure she wasn't hiding nearby. He looked around for other prey. But all the animals and Beck were safely out of sight.

Out of ideas, the hawk gave up and flew away.

All around the clearing, the animals breathed sighs of relief. They had outwitted the hawk. They had saved Nan and Twitter.

And they had done it by working together.

10

THE ANIMALS STAYED hidden for a few minutes to make sure the coast was really clear. Then, one by one, chipmunks, mice, hummingbirds, sparrows, chickadees, moles, and cardinals came out of their hiding places. Slowly and warily, they gathered in the clearing. They made a wide circle around Nan and Twitter, Uncle Munk, Birdie, and Beck.

"Are you two all right?" Beck asked the youngsters. They looked unharmed. But Beck could sense that they were still getting over their fear — especially Nan.

"I'm okay," Twitter replied.

He was strangely calm — none of his usual flitting around. Maybe this *real* emergency had sapped all his nervous energy, thought Beck. If so, the change was sure to be temporary. Beck expected he'd be back to his old excitable self in no time.

"Are *you* okay, Nan?" Twitter asked his new friend. Beck translated for him.

Nan nodded but didn't speak.

"She'll be fine," Uncle Munk said cheerfully. He looked up at Birdie. "And it's thanks to you, old bird. What would we have done if you hadn't stepped in and saved her?" Uncle Munk looked down at the ground bashfully. "You risked everything for Nan. How can we thank you?"

Beck told Birdie what Uncle Munk had said. Birdie brushed off the praise with a wave of her wing. "Nonsense," she replied. "*You're* the one who got Twitter safely out of that log. You are due as much credit as I am." She turned to Beck. "And you! What if you hadn't been here, Beck? We were all so wrapped up in our" — Birdie paused — "*argument*. We might not have seen that the little ones were in trouble. . .until it was too late."

Beck smiled a big smile. Her glow flared with a mixture of embarrassment and pride. "Oh, don't mention it," she said. But secretly, Beck was very glad to think she might have been of some help. Especially after days and days of trying to end the Berry Battle — with no luck.

"I'm just glad this whole thing is over," Beck said with a chuckle. She looked at Uncle Munk. She looked at Birdie. Her chuckle trailed off. "It *is* over, isn't it?" she asked them, first in Chipmunk, then in Bird. "The Berry Battle, I mean."

Birdie shifted her weight from one foot

to the other. "Well," she said, "there *is* the small matter of the nest." She looked over at Uncle Munk. "The missing nest, that is. I *do* think it would be nice if they would return it."

Uncle Munk stared at Beck with wide eyes while she translated. "But we didn't even take that nest!" he cried. "Honestly! I don't know why they think we did."

Birdie squinted at Uncle Munk. She was trying to decide whether she believed him. Uncle Munk stared back at her. Beck hovered nervously between them. *Oh, no,* she thought. *Here we go again.*

No one spoke for many long moments. The whole clearing was silent. All the other animals waited to hear what would happen next.

Then, on the outer ring of the circle of

animals, there was a slight commotion.

"Oh, pardon me," came a friendly voice from the midst of the hubbub.

Beck watched as the animals in that area shifted suddenly to the left and to the right. They seemed to be clearing a path for someone.

"Oh, excuse me," said the voice. "Oof! Pardon me. Oh! Bit of a gathering here, eh?"

The front row of animals parted. Out from behind them strolled old Grandfather Mole. He had stumbled and bumped his way through the crowd. Now, moseying past Beck, he tipped his hat. "Good day, sir!" he said to her. "Somewhat crowded in the forest today, isn't it?"

It took a few moments for Beck to notice that his hat was not a hat at all. It was an upside-down, hollowed-out mass of moss, plant bits, and spiderwebs.

It was a hummingbird nest.

"Um, Grandfather Mole?" she called. She flew over and landed facing him. "If you please," she said, "where did you get that. . . *thing* on your head?"

All around Beck, the animals realised what it was. They gasped and pointed at Grandfather Mole's head. Birdie's beak hung open.

"What?" Grandfather Mole said. "Do you mean my hat?" He reached up and took it off. He held it out at arm's length. He squinted at it. "Isn't it a fine hat? I found it a few days ago. I was out for a walk. I strolled by that blackberry bush over yonder." Grandfather Mole pointed to the hummingbirds' bush — the very bush that the missing nest had been in.

"This hat was on the ground underneath it. Oh, naturally, I looked around to see if anyone might have dropped it. But there was no one in sight. So I picked it up and tried it on. It fit perfectly!" He put the nest back on his head. "See?" he said, modelling it for Beck. "I'm wearing it out for the first time this afternoon. With all this strange weather we've been having, it's come in very handy," Grandfather Mole added.

Beck could not believe her ears. She looked over at Birdie and Uncle Munk. They seemed equally amazed. Could it be? Had the nest actually just *fallen* out of the bush? Had Grandfather Mole had it the whole time? Had the forest really been divided over a silly misunderstanding?

"Well, good day to you," said Grand-father Mole as he continued on his walk. He strolled out of the clearing. The animals watched him walk away with a hummingbird nest on his head.

Then, suddenly, Beck and all the animals — hummingbirds, chipmunks, moles, mice, sparrows, chickadees, and cardinals — began to laugh.

They laughed because they hadn't laughed in days. They laughed at their memories of each other dripping in berry juice. They laughed from relief that it was over. And they laughed because Grandfather Mole looked very silly with a nest for a hat.

Their laughter was so loud that several Never fairies in the Home Tree, a fair distance away, heard the sound.

It was the sound of the end of the Berry Battle.